BACHELOR HEART

A RICH INDULGENCE NOVEL

REGINA MORRIS

Silkhaven Publishing, LLC
Join Regina Morris' mailing list for games, freebies, and fun at http://newsletter.reginamorris.com
Please visit author Regina Morris on her website http://www.reginamorris.com
Regina Morris enjoys connecting with fans on social media. Please find her at:
Facebook: http://www.facebook.com/ReginaAnnMorris (@ReginaMorris)
Twitter: http://www.twitter.com/ReginaMorris (@ReginaMorris)
Pinterest: http://www.pinterest.com/ReginaAnnMorris

Deborah Baxter, personal assistant to a powerful CEO, never expected her boss would want her to pose as his fake fiancée. She is plenty attracted to him, but she's a 38 year-old single mother—now turned empty-nester—who hasn't dated in years. Does she really want to go on romantic dates with her boss at the city's glitziest spots? She says yes anyway.

At 49, Daniel Ellington has everything a billionaire could want—except maybe romantic happiness. And that's only because he doesn't really want it—there's much to be said about shallow affairs when you are a busy man. But now reliable sources are telling him he is about to be named one of the country's ten most eligible bachelors by People Magazine, and that kind of tabloid attention is the last thing he wants. Having his assistant pose a his fiancée seems to be the ideal answer, at least at first.

Their whirlwind fake—or is it real—romance explodes on social media. The loss of privacy drives Daniel nuts. But these troubles are nothing compared to Deborah's refusal to date him for real. What is his assistant keeping secret? And more importantly, how can he change her mind?

Silkhaven Publishing, LLC

ISBN: 978–1–948997–53–9 (EPub Ebook)

ISBN: 978–1–948997–54–6 (MOBI Ebook)

ISBN: 978–1–948997–55–3 (Paperback)

Library of Congress Control Number: 2021915032

Copyright (c) 2021 Regina Morris

(V1) – July 22, 2021

 Created with Vellum

1

"I can't make next week's meeting." Daniel Ellington sat in the Green Terrace Country Club with his two best friends and enjoyed their pact —breakfast once a week with no mention of work. No medical technologies that were on the horizon from Ravi; no interesting cases from Scott, the lawyer. Daniel scooped up some eggs on his fork and allowed the peaceful dining hall to be his oasis from the craziness of work.

"Just as well. I might have a medical conference next week." Ravi then waved dismissively. "I'm not sure I'll go. My last trip had a two-hour delay due to bad weather." He then glanced over to Scott. "I guess you and Caroline aren't going anywhere for a while."

The one topic that seemed central to their weekly meals had been the subject of Scott's blessed arrival. His baby was due soon, and it was all the man could talk about. Daniel shot Ravi a stern gaze, one that Ravi picked up on and sheepishly mouthed the word, 'sorry'.

Scott's face beamed with pride, which usually launched him into a rendition of how happy he was in holy married bliss with a baby on the way. "Caroline shouldn't travel this late into her pregnancy."

Daniel didn't appreciate the topic change. Everyone who was married seemed to have no problems finding the woman of their dreams. Men seemed to forget how difficult the dating scene was on their journey to find the right person. "Yeah, yeah. Marriage is great. We get it, Scott."

"Marriage makes no sense," Ravi said.

"Hey, trust me." Scott focused on both men at the table. "If you can find a woman who can put up with your shit, you need to keep her."

Ravi let out a huff, as though he had heard the advice too many times. "Well, Caroline kept you off the list, so it's a good thing you married her."

Scott's jaw tightened. "I married her because I love her, not because of that stupid list."

Ravi shook his head and took another bite of his meal, creating a silence between the three men. Daniel set down his fork. "What list?"

With an evil grin, Ravi said, "That's right. You weren't living in Chicago last year." He let out a slight chuckle, a chuckle that held a secret. Using his fork to point over to Daniel, he asked, "Have you noticed more reporters hanging around your office lately?"

There were two reporters just this morning that had followed him into his office building. "Maybe," Daniel said, his voice filled with trepidation. He sipped his coffee and wondered why both his friends looked as if he had just stepped on a land mind.

"And have they been hanging around your home?" Scott asked, leaning in and looking intrigued.

With his friends being a doctor and lawyer, you'd think they'd have a better way of telling someone bad news. They knew something—something unpleasant. "Reporters are frickin' everywhere. I don't mind press conferences, but lately, they've been more of a nuisance." Daniel gingerly picked at his eggs as he thought about how many newshounds he had bumped into recently, even on the sidewalk outside his favorite restaurant. Taking a minute to focus on other encounters, he said, "Several have been hanging around the lobby of my office and around my house. They're even bothering my assistant."

Could information about the merger have leaked out? Was there a list of stocks to buy? Or worse, a list to avoid? Daniel had been so careful and only a handful of people knew.

"It's that time again," Scott nodded to Ravi, a shifty stare in his eyes. "No single man is safe."

Daniel head ping-ponged from Scott to Ravi. He hated games, so he buttered a slice of toast and pretended that their joint secret didn't upset him. He pointed to the jelly across the table. "What are you talking about?" he calmly asked.

"Chicago's Top 10 Bachelor list," Scott said in an ominous tone. "They announce the list every year soon after Valentine's Day."

"Sort of like open season on all of us single men," Ravi handed the basket of little jars of jelly to Daniel. "The ladies of Chicago take the list seriously. Probably only half the men listed for one year will make it on to next year's list because they all scramble to get married."

"Less than half," Scott said.

Daniel's toast dropped to the plate. A fucking manhunt? Daniel felt the air leave the room and his heartbeat—thunderous and loud—echoed within his ears and threatened to explode from his chest. He didn't want—no didn't need—this type of publicity. "Who qualifies to be on this list?"

"The richest single men living in Chicago," Scott said.

"In other words," Ravi said, his eyes narrowing in on him. "You."

Damn. That explained the photographers over the last week disturbing his evenings with his girlfriend Brandelynn, taking their picture and following them all around town. He didn't need this crap, especially since things with Brandelynn were, at best, shaky.

The room suddenly got warm. "I don't want to be

on any damn list. Can I pay someone to keep me off it?"

"You're not the only one who's had that idea. It won't work," Ravi said through a fit of laughter. He pointed over to Scott. "He tried to pay his way off last year."

Daniel's gaze darted over. His friend was an heir to the Hollister Hotel fortune and senior partner in the most successful law firm in Chicago, representing the richest clients. He even had an office in Daniel's building. "How much did you…?"

Scott shook his head. "Bribes don't work."

Money always worked for Daniel. It was his fallback position with no exceptions. "But wait. You're married with a baby on the way. How could you even be listed?"

"I wasn't married a year ago. It's only been eleven months."

The wedding wasn't even a year ago? Thinking back, the event had happened just before Daniel had moved his business to Chicago. He had known Scott for decades, but the man's marriage felt longer since Scott managed to mention his wife in nearly every sentence around the office.

Daniel was searching for a high-class woman, not a high maintenance one. This list would have every gold-digger and opportunist coming after him. The desperate and the crazies would come out looking for him—again. His entire life, he had done his best to keep his personal life out of the press.

He was screwed.

He let out a deep sigh, one that Charlie Brown would envy.

Pushing around some fruit with his fork, he thought for a moment. Even with the constant mention of marital bliss from Scott, the two were a great couple. "You and Caroline were dating for a while. Did this list have anything to do with you proposing?"

"I'd planned to ask her to marry me anyway, but the list sped up the process."

Ravi, Scott's friend that Daniel had met once moving to Chicago, was a professed bachelor—someone that Daniel could relate to.

The doctor grimaced. "Women were coming out of the woodwork wanting to date Scott. Didn't one jump in front of your car so she could meet you?"

Scott closed his eyes and let out a deep breath. "Yep. And one trapped herself in an elevator with me, and one was a flight attendant wanting me to fly her friendly skies, and one pretended to be my mailman who had a special delivery for me." He let out a groan and looked at his friends. "All were after one thing— a rich husband and his wallet. With this list, it's like you have a bull's-eye on your back for several weeks."

"The women will come out of thin air,

surrounding you until you can't even breathe," Ravi said, shuddering. "I'm glad I'm not on it." His voice sounded decisive, as if the line had been drawn in the sand and no desperate bimbo bride could cross it. "And, you know what? There is no Top 10 Bachelorette list. The whole thing is sexist."

What a god–awful thing. You work hard, make money and produce a product that people need… and they repay you by making you fair game for every scam artist in the world.

Daniel shifted in his seat, pulling his suit jacket around him tighter. The room suddenly felt claustrophobic, and he took a deep breath to steady himself. "Other than being rich, what else does it take to be listed?" Daniel asked as nonchalantly as he could while snatching a strip of bacon from Scott's plate. It was one of his many comfort foods that he was certain Ravi, as his doctor, took note of.

Ravi let out a *pfft* sound. "Don't worry. You'll be listed. They'll wrap you up and serve you to the masses with a big red bow."

"You'll probably be in the top three." Scott scooted his plate farther away from Daniel. "You make more money than Ravi and I combined." Scott finished off his coffee. "A good–looking, rich man like you will definitely be brought to the slaughter. But there is one sure–fire way to get off the list."

A glimmer of hope surrounded Daniel. There was a way to be safe.

"Two," Ravi said, correcting him.

Scott thought for a moment. "Two ways. But the first way is much more fun."

"Eeeccchh," Ravi's face bunched together as though he'd just eaten a lemon. "Personally, I'd rather not take what's behind door number one."

To Daniel it was like watching a verbal badminton match where the bird fluttered down way too slowly. There was a way out, and he needed to know the escape routes. "You two want to share with the whole class?"

Scott gave a sneaky, devilish, an I-told-you-so type of evil grin. "Strap on the ball-and-chain." He tapped his finger on the table and emphasized each word of, "Best decision I ever made."

"Or," Ravi said, "You can sell your house and move out of the city since you have to live in Chicago to be listed."

"Moving is such a hassle," Scott said.

"And a wedding isn't?" Ravi said, challenging Scott.

Scott's eyebrow rose, and he seemed willing to accept the challenge. "Look, having a wife is…"

"Wait." Daniel didn't need another one of Scott's persuasive talks about the joys of marriage, and by the look Ravi was giving him, Ravi was far from eager to hear it, as well.

"I'm not moving." Daniel's hand went up. "It took my assistant over six months to find my home. It has a helicopter pad on the roof and a beautiful topiary garden and an acre of land. Plus, I have a bowling alley in the basement."

"You're bowling?" Ravi asked.

The bowling alley was installed by the previous owners. Daniel hadn't yet tried either of the two lanes, but he liked that he had the option to do so if the mood struck him.

Knowing how much he didn't like bowling, the mood to play would have to hit him pretty damn hard, so he gave his friends a WTF look as if they should already know the answer.

"Whatever. I got on the top ten list days before it was published because candidates nine and ten became engaged at the last minute," Scott said. "I felt honored until the manhunt began. It didn't end until I proposed to Caroline."

Ravi grabbed a slice of toast and scooped up the remains of the runny yolk on his plate. "You've been dating Brandelynn for a while now. You going to go with option number one?"

Daniel always believed that one day he would get married, but as each year passed the likelihood of that happening waned. He loved spending time with Brandelynn, and really wanted her to be *the one*, but something was holding the relationship back.

He couldn't put his finger on what the problem was. It wasn't anything Brandelynn was doing wrong. The hesitation came from his gut feeling that something stood between them. She was always checking her phone, active on social media, or... he felt she kept secrets from him, but he couldn't explain why he felt like that.

They had mind-numbingly boring interaction by day followed by hot sex at night. Things between them felt bathtub-shallow, and now that he was turning forty, what he wanted in a relationship was more of an ocean depth.

His two best friends should know better than to ask such a pointed question. They stared at him, awaiting his answer—but he didn't know what to say. Any man would be thrilled to be dating a woman nearly half his age. Daniel just didn't feel so lucky. Not anymore.

"No," Daniel said, the tone of his voice sounding defeated. "I won't be taking option number one." He had tried so hard to have things work out with Brandelynn, but she wasn't the love of his life—if there were such a thing—and the relationship, unfortunately, had probably run its course.

It surprised him how sad the revelation made him feel. "I'm thinking of breaking up with her tonight."

Scott laughed. "You can't break up with her today. Did you forget it's Valentine's Day?"

"Rookie move," Ravi said.

"Shit." Daniel couldn't be *that* guy. He dropped his fork and felt like a sledge hammer hit him dead center in the chest. "It's fucking Valentine's Day?" He grabbed his phone and texted his executive assistant, his thumbs dancing across the tiny keypad.

"What's wrong? Your girl needs a fake id?" Ravi asked.

Scott grabbed the salt. "Cut Daniel some slack. She's not that young." He touched Daniel's arm. "Don't take her across the state lines, though."

Daniel ignored the comment and kept texting. "My assistant asked all week about dinner reservations for tonight, and I never put two and two together." He glanced at his friends once he was done with his message and had sent it. "Business has me preoccupied, I guess. I'm running from one crisis to the next." He let out a slight chuckle. "Sometimes, I don't see or hear my assistant at all."

"You don't say," Scott said.

His assistant would understand the blunder and make everything perfect for the evening, she was always good at last-minute details. He waited a minute and then a ding sounded on his phone. The incoming message indicated that everything would be taken care of, including the expensive gift, the dinner reservations, and the car by this evening.

He let out a sigh of relief, and then in a proud voice showing that he had the best employee in the world, Daniel said, "Everything is taken care of."

Ravi glanced at his watch. "Fast and efficient, especially this early in the morning. You wouldn't be interested in loaning your assistant out, would you?"

"I'd be lost without her," Daniel said, knowing how true the statement was. Deborah had been with him for years and knew his routine so well. She understood his schedule, knew how to organize his day, and, above all else, was someone he enjoyed spending time with.

Scott wiped his mouth with a napkin. "Why do you want to break up with Brandelynn?"

As if high-beam lights were thrust upon him and he had to rat-out a dirty boss, Daniel's gaze darted between his two best friends. Privacy was golden, especially private, embarrassing matters.

"It doesn't matter." He needed a plan to stay off the Top 10 list. It was always best to stay out of the limelight, away from the peering eyes of the paparazzi, and far away from the tabloid fodder. He was still stinging from the last time he'd been in the public eye. That was a mess he never wanted to live through again.

The waitress opened the door to the private room and carried in a tray of drinks. "Are your meals all right?"

"They're fine, Kaylee," Daniel said, his voice sounding pre-occupied and reflecting his mood.

Kaylee had been their waitress for the last several months, and knew how to keep orders straight. She understood how to engage them in conversation without being too intrusive, as well.

After filling Daniel's water glass, she reached for

Scott's. "How is that wife of yours Mr. Hollister? Is she still having problems sleeping?"

"Caroline stays up reading to pass the time." Scott's smile and head nod made him look like an expert in the field of late trimester women, and he was only expecting his first child.

Kaylee rubbed her rounded baby bump. "I can't sleep now either, and I know it'll be worse when my baby comes." She gazed over to Scott. "What does Mrs. Hollister enjoy reading?"

"She's found a new romance author that she can't put down."

Ravi rolled his eyes. "Women and romance. They always want a ring on their finger." He glanced up at Kaylee who—thankfully—ignored the comment.

Scott began talking about the best diaper bag and some baby schedule that Daniel wasn't interested in. He let the words trail off as he took a sip of his coffee and then scooted his chair out. "I need to go to the office."

He pulled his wallet from his back pocket so he could leave Kaylee a tip. He thumbed through the bills. Nearly taking out a twenty, he paused and thought about her unborn baby. She'd give birth soon and be unable to work for a while. She'd hurt financially from a lack of tips while on maternity leave. He then chose a one–hundred–dollar bill and set it on the table.

2

Rain pelted Deborah Baxter's car until she turned into the safe haven of the parking garage, which was adjacent to the Ellington–Weston building.

Her phone chirped so she sat in her parked car and read the text from her boss, Mr. Ellington. She knew he had forgotten about Valentine's Day.

There had been a chance that he would have broken up with his current ladylove before today. His new love interest, like all of the women of his past, wasn't a good fit for him. Too selfish. Too greedy. Too… young.

Deborah never understood what he saw in his dates, other than their dumber-than-dirt minds, and their nearly-Barbie-perfect bodies. But she had no room to judge. She certainly wasn't making any big strides in the love department.

The *love department*—she scoffed at the thought. Closed. Sealed. Nonexistent. There was only one man who resided in her heart, and he never dated his employees.

Her phone chirped again, reminding her of Daniel's text. Deborah strove to be two steps ahead of the man's needs, but it was unusual for him to be in a relationship on Valentine's Day.

She placed the first of two important calls, wanting to do her best to make Daniel happy. One for a restaurant reservation, the other for a chauffeured car.

It always impressed her how just mentioning Mr. Ellington's name opened doors in this town. A few minutes later, she had the last seat at the best table the five–star restaurant and a town car.

Crisis averted.

Again.

She texted Mr. Ellington an update on his plans for the evening, a smug smile on her face.

She wouldn't let anything ruin her day, not even the romantic dinner for two she had just set up for her boss.

She tossed her gym bag into the back seat and noticed the bank receipt still lying on the passenger seat. The gym, errands, and already her boss's hero?

Yeah, she was on a roll.

She dashed from the parking garage to her office

building with her umbrella protecting her against getting drenched.

Her sneakers squished against the tile floor as she entered and walked up to security.

"Good morning, Deborah." The security officer pressed the entry button to allow her access. "How is Josh doing in college?"

How was her son doing? He seemed to be having the time of his life with his new friends, new adventures, and new life. Other than a weekly call from him, she hardly heard any news—except when he needed more money, and she had to race to the bank—like this morning—to transfer funds into his account.

"He's doing well," Deborah said through a fake smile. Nobody ever asked how she was coping with empty–nest syndrome, living alone for the first time, and having all her money going off to college with her son.

She took the elevator to the top floor and then walked to her private office. She brushed the rain from her coat before hanging the wet garment on the rack and then shook out her umbrella and placed it in the shiny copper stand next to the door. She then raked her fingers through her slightly wet brunette hair and shook out her damp curls.

She straightened her knockoff designer skirt and adjusted her blouse before digging her high heels from her bag.

Swapping out the New Balance running shoes she wore for her stilettos, she stowed her bag in the filing cabinet.

Before locking the drawer, she studied the tiny cache of gifts. She removed a tiny, wrapped box from Buccellati jewelers from the selection. Thank God, Mr. Ellington trusted her with a personal credit card or she'd be scrambling to find a last–minute gift for his girlfriend, as well.

Yep. Always two steps ahead of the man.

A wicked grin spread across Deborah's lips. Usually, these gifts were parting trinkets. A thanks-for-playing-now-you-have-to-leave bit of gaudy bling to placate the neuron-deficient bimbos.

Deborah felt certain that the latest bimbo du jour was about to receive her gift.

Her desk phone rang, and Deborah glanced at the clock on the wall, a stern look appearing on her face. Reporters had discovered her work number and called several times yesterday about a bachelor list—as if she had time for such frivolity.

It seemed rather early for a business call, but still, she answered it in the same sing-song voice and greeting she always did. After eighteen years, it needed to be a recording.

"Mr. Ellington's office."

"Caroline Hollister is at the front security desk for you, Ms. Baxter."

The sick feeling of having, yet again, to tear

someone a new one left… and Deborah felt a calmness overcoming her as the scowl on her face spread into a giant smile.

"Thank you. Please let her up."

Since Scott was having breakfast with her boss, she could enjoy a little time with her new best friend as she tidied up the office and prepared for the day.

Making a quick trip down the hall, she picked up the day's mail, inter-office envelopes, and the morning newspaper. She placed the pile on the edge of her desk to be sorted later and then walked into Mr. Ellington's interior office.

The slight scent of his cologne—rugged and manly—lingered in the air. She inhaled deeply and knew that the fragrance likely came from Daniel's jacket, which hung on the back of his leather chair.

She picked up the fine wool garment and brushed it out with her hand. He'd probably ask her to take it to the cleaners, so she draped it over her arm so she could place it next to her purse later. She then found the remote for the window, so she opened the blinds and allowed the sparse sunshine of the day to stream inside.

"Deborah?" Caroline walked into the outer office, a plastic visitors badge swinging from a chain around her neck.

Deborah peered out of her boss's office and motioned for the woman to come in. "Caroline, dear. How are you feeling?"

A slight injured-sea-lion of a moan escaped. "Fat."

Caroline wore a new coat sized extra-large to fit her round frame. Deborah's heart went out to her. "You're nearly nine months along and absolutely glowing. No one sees you as fat."

She removed her wet coat. "That's sweet of you to say, but I couldn't put my shoes on today."

The two looked down at Caroline's flat, white Keds and her Fred Flintstone sized swollen feet and ankles.

"Have a seat." Deborah motioned for the chair in front of her desk.

"It'll be another quiet evening at home for me and Scott, not that I'd be interested in going out and dancing tonight or anything." Caroline positioned her arms on the chair and slowly sat herself down.

"Trust me, once the baby comes, you'll wish you had more quiet evenings at home." Deborah hung the wet coat on a nearby coat rack, and placed Daniel's jacket on the hook beside it. "What brings you downtown so early?"

Caroline rubbed her belly. "Weekly doctor appointments until the big day gets here." She glanced out the window at the clouds preventing the sun from shining through. "I was a bit too early, so I came here to escape the weather."

"It is dreadful." Deborah heard a slight clap of thunder off in the distance, one that threatened even more rain. It was an ugly and depressing Valentine's Day.

Deborah moved the stack of papers so Caroline could set down her purse, and a large insert fell from the newspaper. It was the society column. Deborah saw several wedding announcements. There always seemed to be more of them occurring around Valentine's Day than any other holiday.

The quality portraits captured the hope and dreams within warm smiles and twinkling eyes. She reminded herself not to be so cynical, and she placed the insert back into the paper. She shouldn't step on someone else's happiness, even if she was raising a child on her own and was an old maid.

"Coffee?"

"Decaf, please." Caroline's flat tone was that of a woman desperate for caffeine. "What are you doing tonight? Are you seeing anyone special?"

The questions seemed simple enough, but Caroline knew Deborah wasn't dating anyone. The subject had come up twice over the last week—as if it were a crime to spend Valentine's Day alone, especially if it was your birthday. You can't choose the day of your birth, but having the two forever entwined was a cruel curse.

"We've already discussed that topic." Deborah made her way to the small corridor that connected her office with Mr. Ellington's. It held a coffee bar service with the finest Kruger coffeemaker money could buy.

While Caroline rattled off the joys of being in a healthy relationship, and how everyone should be so happy, Deborah made some coffee and allowed Caroline's voice to trail off to a background hum, easy to ignore.

"That all sounds wonderful for you, Caroline." Happiness came from within, and Deborah didn't want or need a man to make her happy. She finished with the coffee and handed the decaf to Caroline.

"I just don't understand why a beautiful woman like you isn't dating."

It was kind of her to say so, but it was like an mp3 file playing in a loop—a loop that needed to end.

"Some people just weren't made for marriage." Deborah's voice was distant as she turned to her computer and logged into her profile. She needed to sort through the company's Slack feed, Mr. Ellington's personal emails and phone messages, as well as any Skype discussions.

"You don't really believe that some people aren't the marriage type, do you?"

She didn't, but it gave her the strength to give up on ever finding a man of her own. "Old Maids and Confirmed Bachelors are terms for a reason."

Deborah's computer showed that the trending hashtag for the city was #top10bachelors. That explained the many phone calls she received yesterday from reporters. She had thought their interest was in another security breakthrough by the company, but all they wanted to do was harass her boss.

"What do you know about this Top 10 Bachelor list?" Deborah asked.

"It's a list of the richest single men in the city. It's an annual thing some cities do."

It sounded rather barbaric to Deborah, but judging by the social media hits on the topic, she figured people were interested in such things.

"I think it was one reason Scott proposed to me. You see, he made it on last year's list."

"Did he?" Deborah hadn't realized Scott was one of the richest men in Chicago, but, overall, it didn't surprise her since the man was a senior partner in a successful law firm. And, if she remembered correctly, his family came from money.

"The city goes crazy. Women were after Scott like he was a PEZ dispenser shooting out money. Our engagement stopped most of them from bothering him. Which reminds me...you never answered my question. What you are doing tonight?"

"Me?" Couldn't Caroline just let the topic rest? It was bad enough knowing that Daniel would be out with his child of a girlfriend; Deborah didn't need to be reminded that she would be alone— again. "I am spending the evening at my sister's house. Her husband is deployed so she'll be alone tonight."

"I didn't realize you had a sister in the city."

Deborah glanced at the pile of today's mail on her desk that needed sorting. "Not quite downtown Chicago, but close enough."

"Well," Caroline said, her voice stretching out the word like a huge imposition would follow. "The main reason I came to visit… is to set you up on a date with someone."

"Me?" Deborah's heart skipped a beat, and not in a good way. She sipped her coffee, needing a pause in the conversation. "You want to set me up on a blind date?"

"Consider it your birthday gift."

So, Caroline did remember, and right now the smile on her face had a this–is–a–gift–you–can't–return look. "You don't have to give me a present…"

"But I found the perfect man for you, and I want you to meet him."

That wasn't going to happen. Deborah was already trying to adjust to one major life change; she didn't want to take on another. "Perhaps once Josh is settled more in college…"

"He's been gone nearly six months."

It felt much longer. "I'm not ready. Maybe in a little while…"

"Deborah…"

Deborah nodded to the clock on the wall. "When

did you say your appointment was?" Her heart raced and she needed some alone time. Everything in her life was settled, and she wanted to enjoy the peace and quiet. Why would she want a man to be thrown into the mix?

3

A horde of press surrounded Daniel as he entered the Ellington–Weston building. Microphones were shoved in his face and crossing his boundary level of comfort.

"Mr. Ellington, any comments on the Top Ten list?" a few of the reporters shouted.

Another asked, "What is your dating status? Are you proposing tonight to your long-term girlfriend?"

"No comment." His body tightened and he quickened his pace, weaving his way through the crowd to the front security desk. He wondered exactly when dating someone casually for six months qualified as a "long term" girlfriend.

The term "girlfriend" bothered him more than the suggested duration. Daniel wanted to share his life with someone, but he feared Brandelynn was a far cry from what he sought. He gave a nod to the security officer, and the man buzzed him through.

"Sorry about the press, Mr. Ellington. Evidently, there is some sort of bachelor news article." His hand waved dismissively to the crowd. "I asked them to leave, but, you know, freedom of the press."

"Understood." Daniel glanced back at the crowd, who still shouted questions at him. His stomach twisted, and he knew he needed to escape the sea of people. "Make sure they don't get past the lobby of the building."

"Yes, sir?" The security guard studied him cautiously. "Are you all right, sir? You look a little pale."

"I'm fine," Daniel squeaked out. He took a quick deep breath, feeling his lungs fully expand, and his body slightly shiver. Crowds, especially when all eyes were on him, unnerved him.

Press conferences, company workshops, employee retreats... Work-related events were one thing. He could handle them. People were more interested in the announcement of the business news than with him personally, and he never felt like a target when representing his companies.

The security guard nodded. "Have a good day, sir."

Daniel managed his way to the elevator. He took in a deep breath, enjoying the security and peace of the rest of the building. His racing heart rate slowed, and he wiped the sweat from his brow.

He was safe.

He now focused on the elegant, marble–tiled floors, the shiny metal elevator doors, and the soft, gentle music that played in the background. His surrounding centered him and brought him back to the present. He wasn't a scared six-year-old boy, snatched from his parents. He was a grown man, and a powerful one at that.

This grand building was his haven, and he was the master of his domain.

The office complex showcased his latest accomplishment. He'd taken a small, nearly fading–into–the–distance company and, within just five years, made it into what was now listed as a Fortune 500. His nickname should be Midas, for he certainly had the golden touch.

Once upstairs in his corner office, and far away from the crowd downstairs, he found his coffee and newspaper. Everything in its place. Everything where it needed to be.

His body relaxed and he felt at home. Ms. Baxter remained on top of things, as usual, and it was time to get to work.

He removed paperwork from his briefcase, and before he could even ask for Ms. Baxter to come into the room, he smelled her perfume. He didn't know the name of the fragrance, never cared to ask, but it was distinctly *Deborah.*

Already standing behind him, she greeted him. "Good morning, Mr. Ellington. Your ten o'clock appointment will be here in thirty minutes." She walked closer to him and helped him off with his jacket. "I'll place Mr. Covington in the conference room once he arrives." She walked to the wooden valet stand in the corner and put the jacket on the hanger.

Pleasantly professional. Calm and cordial. What was it about Deborah that centered Daniel and made him feel safe? For nearly twenty years, she had been his rock. She knew the structure of the office and seemed to anticipate his every move.

She set some paperwork on his desk and placed his coffee mug back on the coaster, her hips swaying as she moved effortlessly around his desk and tidied up.

Daniel's father's words echoed in his mind: *"Never fish off the company pier."* It was the number-one rule his father had stressed when Daniel joined the business decades ago—one that he upheld no matter what.

He moved his gaze from her bottom and stared out the window instead. Ms. Baxter was a perfect *work wife*, and nothing more.

She could never be anything other than that.

Ever.

Still standing at the corner of his desk, she cleared her throat to get his attention— waiting for her next assignment.

This morning's meeting was with the CEO of Pinksley Inc., a sizeable company, but not truly a competitor for Daniel's business. Still a nice asset from a business acquisition, though.

"Ms. Baxter, I'll need…"

"Mr. Covington's company's folder." She gestured to Daniel's desk, a teasing smile on her face. "I've already brought it in. As well as your paper, your coffee, and the little present we discussed this morning."

Daniel took a seat and noticed a gift lying squarely on top of the folder. Its delicate red bow in place, and the gift card, already typed out with his sentiments ready for him. "Thanks for taking care of this." He picked up the present and moved it aside.

The outside phone line rang, causing Ms. Baxter to walk toward the door. "I'll be right back, sir."

He heard the familiar, "Mr. Ellington's office" greeting she always recited. She always sounded so professional on the phone, but today, irritation sounded in her voice.

"I'm sorry for the interruption, sir," she said as she joined him back in his office.

He glanced at her. "Something wrong?"

In a mildly irritated tone, she said, "The phone keeps ringing. Evidently, there is a list…"

Holding up his hand, he stopped her mid-sentence. He understood how reporters were now distracting her. "I know. Try to keep the interruptions to a minimum."

"Of course, sir."

The press should be focused on the company's new software suite, not the stupid Top 10 Bachelor list. But he didn't have time for that right now. He had to focus on his ten o'clock meeting.

The outside phone rang again. Even though Daniel preferred it open, he said, "Please, shut the door." He realized Ms. Baxter was already heading out of the room saying, "Of course, sir."

4

*D*aniel glanced out the living room window of his home and checked for his ride—again. Seeing lights off in the distance, he pushed a button on his phone to open his iron security gate, giving the car entry onto his private property.

An evening out. He didn't have time for Valentine's Day and needed to focus on the merger instead. He straightened his tie and adjusted his coat, making sure Brandelynn's gift still lay inside his breast pocket, before walking outside.

He had a minute, so he gave her a call. "Hello, sweetheart," he said once she picked up. "I'll be there in a few minutes. I'll come up to your condo and get…"

"That's sweet of you, but I'll meet you outside in front of the building," Brandelynn replied over the phone.

"It's no bother."

She paused before adding, *"I need to finish getting ready. I'll meet you downstairs, darling."*

He stared at his phone after she abruptly hung up. She had hinted before that she was a slob and the state of her home embarrassed her. Still, he felt odd about her insisting they meet downstairs all the time.

The car pulled up, and it wasn't exactly what he expected, but this entire evening felt off to him. The vehicle seemed smaller than he normally rode in, but he figured he had no right to complain with such a last–minute accommodation.

A young man stepped out of the car. He had a humbling, I'm-here-to-serve-you smile and a snappy pressed suit that stressed a serious first impression.

"Good evening, sir." He dashed over to open Daniel's door. "My name is Evan, and I'll be your chauffeur tonight. I understand we will be picking up your guest for the evening. I have the address."

Chatty, professional, and pimply-faced.

Daniel usually didn't like overly–friendly staff, but Evan had an Opie-honest look, a large hat that didn't fit, and no hand extended for a tip.

Daniel remembered himself at that age—eager to work and hungry to make his mark on the world.

He got into the car, which felt roomier than he had first thought, and the cleanliness of it impressed him. The only exception was a forgotten magazine that lay half–hidden under the seat in front of him.

"I guess I'm not your first ride this evening." Daniel picked up the copy of *Self–Made Diva* magazine and rolled his eyes once he'd read the cover. The model was one of the Kaiser girls, a wealthy family of actresses—if you could call them that—who were enjoying their fifteen minutes of fame. He had no idea which one was featured on the cover and didn't care.

"I gave two rides earlier tonight, sir." Evan steered the car onto the highway. "But I'll be yours for the rest of the evening. I'll wait outside the restaurant for you." His hand tapped something in the front seat. "I have my advertising and marketing books to study to keep me busy."

Evan seemed like a nice boy. His voice—sincere and respectful—triggered a protective response in Daniel, almost fatherly.

"I'll be dining for a while, so make sure to get something to eat."

Evan held up a small lunch sack. "My wife made me dinner. I'll be all right, sir."

Daniel studied Evan, who seemed too young to be married. The driver reminded him of Ms. Baxter's son, Josh. Courteous, polite, and boy's face that still had to be grown into. "I'm sorry you can't spend Valentine's Day with your wife, but I do appreciate the ride."

"She's disappointed, but understands. We talked it over, and since I earn time and a half driving tonight, taking the night off didn't make sense—especially with a baby on the way."

A baby?

This young man certainly jumped in head first into the responsibility pool. He and his wife "talked it over"? That boded well for the relationship if they treated each other like equal partners. Evan sounded earnest, with the last sentence not a ploy for a bigger tip. A hard–working man who'd lucked out and found an understanding wife who supported him.

Some people were just lucky in love.

Glancing at the cover of the magazine, Daniel read the headline. *"How you know when you've found your soul mate."*

Good Lord. Women bought these types of magazines?

Publications of this sort were a billion-dollar industry, so he thumbed through the perfume-ad laden rag. It was filled with articles about finding "the one."

It was one ridiculous article after the next.

But these magazines sold. And sold well.

Just as he was about to toss the magazine aside, he asked, "Evan, you're a married man. Would you say your wife is your soul mate?"

Through the rear-view mirror, Daniel could see the young man smiling.

"She's my whole world, sir." His voice sounded genuine, not sappy and silly. He really did believe his wife was 'the one'.

"How long have you been married?"

"Two years. I just knew she was the love of my life and had to propose. You know, 'the one'"

And there it was again—"the one."

Daniel smiled at Evan and then looked down at the magazine, dismissing the boy so he could focus on driving.

The magazine seemed more geared toward women finding their Mr. Rights, but Daniel figured he could somehow reverse engineer the process and have the information still help him.

After a few minutes, he finished reading the feature article and memorized the top three bullet points—take an interest in what your partner does in the present, know about their childhood and family for their past, and know about their dreams for the future.

Did women talk about such things? He figured they must amongst themselves, but not to the men in their lives. At least, one of the women in his past had every shared such things with him.

He glanced up and watched Evan. If he had to guess, Evan's wife talked to him about such things.

And then a pang of guilt hit Daniel.

The women of *his* life never talked to *him*.

He was the problem.

There was a quiz at the back of the magazine entitled, "Does he really know you?" Since he didn't know Brandelynn that well, and he didn't have a sister, the first female to cross his mind was Ms. Baxter. So, he took the quiz with her in mind.

The questions ranged from personal ambitions to greatest fears and loftiest dreams. Overall, it was quite comprehensive in a twenty-question quiz.

One inquiry in particular surprised him. "Can you get lost in her eyes?" There was no definition of what *lost* mean, or what the significance of being lost was, but Daniel envisioned Ms. Baxter's green eyes nonetheless. They were soft and caring, filled with concern most times, and… compassion at others.

Was it empathy he saw in her eyes?

He paused and thought about it. She occasionally gave him glances where her expression was…? Was it understanding?

Yes. She understood him like no other woman had.

Could he get lost in her eyes?

A fluttering in his gut told him the answer. Yes. She was honest. She was the one woman who wasn't crazy-obsessed with his wealth. She was safe.

Could he get lost in Brandelynn's eyes?

The question haunted him. He wasn't even sure of their color.

Scoring ninety percent on the quiz—using Deborah as the woman—gave Daniel a warm feeling of pride, and that brought a smile to his face. Ms. Baxter wasn't the easiest person to get to know, but once you knew her, she was easy to talk to, easier to trust, and it was effortless to…like her a great deal.

With such a high score, he believed he wasn't such a bastard as the articles would have him believe. He did know at least one woman personally in his life. Of course, he had known her for decades.

He just needed to know Brandelynn better. That's all.

Evan exited the highway and turned down Brandelynn's street.

"My date will be waiting outside." Daniel folded the magazine in half and placed it under his vest. It caused a bit of a bulge, but it was one he could live with. He just didn't want anyone to see him with it.

The car's turn signal blinked, making its click click sound, and Evan steered it into an available parking spot in front of the building.

"Is the woman in the black coat your date, sir?"

Daniel spotted the stylishly dressed, middle-aged woman wearing a full-length coat who stood on the corner of the street. She glanced up and down the street. Her hair held a touch of gray, her curvy waistline wasn't model perfect, and, if he could make out her face, it was creased with wrinkles. Was that the type of woman Evan could see him with?

The woman's face lit up when a man approached and the two walked off together.

"Why did you think she would be with me?"

"You're dressed very elegantly tonight, sir. So was

she." Even from the back seat, Daniel could see Evan beginning to sweat. "A classically beautiful woman like that, her hair all made up, her jewelry very complimentary... Plus, she was waiting for someone. She's what me and my friends call a banana split kind of woman."

"Just pull over here. I'll tell you when I see her." Daniel knew he wasn't up to date with the latest slang, so he had to ask, "Banana split?"

Evan chuckled as he temporarily parked the car, the blinker lights clicking. "It's a silly rating system ranging from a one-scoop up to a banana split, with the top ice cream being a quality woman with good looks, intelligence, and a kind heart."

"Interesting. And that elderly woman was a banana split?"

"I didn't have a chance to meet her, but just going on looks, I'd say she was potentially a banana split."

Daniel pointed to Brandelynn as she walked toward them, her head glancing from side to side since she had not seen them yet. "There she is."

She wore a strapless dress, bright red lipstick, and high heels. Model perfect.

"That's my date." Daniel's voice was full of pride as the two of them watched her check the time and look up and down the road once more.

Evan's eyes widened. "She's very beautiful, sir." His voice sounded flat as he unbuckled his seatbelt. "I'll get her."

No comment on her looks? No 'wow' factor? Even for a man Evan's age Brandelynn was a catch. "You don't see me with someone as smokin' hot as her?"

"It's not my place, sir. And, again, I'm sorry for mistaking her for the other lovely lady."

Daniel felt as though he were being judged, not admired.

He didn't like it.

"What's wrong with my date?"

Evan hesitated, so Daniel asked again, this time adding, "I have plenty of yes-men. I would like an honest opinion, so please tell me the truth."

Even licked his lips and swallowed hard. "I just thought the first woman…"

"The older woman."

The young man took a deep breath and seemed nervous, like his job were on the line. "The first, *older* woman looked classy. Her hair and makeup were flawless and the smile she gave her husband when he picked her up, well, it showed how beautiful she was on the inside."

Brandelynn gave a sour expression as she studied the streets, obviously looking for Daniel's usual limo.

"And my date?" Daniel asked, wondering if Evan could pin point what Daniel knew nagged in the back of his mind but could never fully identify. "What's your take on her?"

Even studied Brandelynn, his gaze moving from

her highlights to her spiked heels. "She's young and beautiful."

"And?"

"Sir. I don't think it's my place to say anything."

Daniel leaned forward so that Evan could turn and look him in the eye instead of through the mirror. "Your honest opinion. I'm really interested."

Evan nodded as he glanced at Brandelynn and then back to Daniel. "She looks upset and cold. I should fetch her for you."

"Evan."

He took a deep breath and let it out slowly. "Honestly, she's trying too hard, she's inappropriately dressed, and she looks like she belongs on a street corner, but not necessarily this one. She's like a sloppy double scoop."

Evan lowered his face and didn't make eye contact with Daniel.

"A double scoop doesn't sound all that bad." Daniel gestured towards his chest as though he held up boobs. "She's a *nice* double scoop."

"Yes," Evan said, letting out a nervous chuckle. "But she's a double scoop of bubble-gum ice cream. Exciting at first, but then you grow up and want something that doesn't leave a bad taste in your mouth."

"Really? You got all that just by glancing at her." Daniel's voice sounded harsher than he had wanted but there were now words to how he was feeling.

Evan was able to size up his problem with Brandelynn just be glancing at her. The boy had potential.

Evan shrunk in his seat. "I'm sorry, sir. She certainly is…beautiful."

Daniel's jaw tightened and he had a feeling of wanting to justify himself to this boy, although he didn't owe the young man anything. Brandelynn was the type of woman to give any man an instant erection. Any man would want to be with her. There was just that underlying current of uncertainty about her that bugged Daniel.

Perhaps if he got to know her better, like the magazine article suggested. Perhaps then she'd check all of his boxes.

"I'm sure she's intelligent and witty and charming. I'm sure you have a wonderful relationship."

The boy was back pedaling.

Daniel reclined back in the seat. "Just go get her."

Evan jumped out of the car and ran toward Brandelynn.

She always stood outside the condo for pickup. Daniel had found it odd, but she was a slob and too embarrassed for him to see where she lived. She also probably preferred his spacious home whenever they were together.

Another article in the magazine suggested that for true intimacy that you need to open your world up to the other person. Perhaps on their next date he could insist that they stay at her place. See how she lived. See her style in decorating. See her world.

Next time.

Of course, her place didn't have the same level of security his home did.

He studied her expression as Evan approached her and introduced himself. She did appear unhappy. She also looked cold. Evan was right, she needed a jacket. Her dress was sexy as hell, but not appropriate. He felt certain she wore the high-cut, low-cleavage outfit just for him, so how could he complain?

Now that Evan had met her, he wondered what else the young man would pick up on.

———————

Evan opened the back-passenger side door. A gust of wind billowed out Brandelynn's dress and her blonde hair draped across her face. She climbed in, her hand clearing the errant strands from her forehead as she shivered.

"You look lovely tonight," Daniel said as he leaned in and kissed her.

"New car?"

It wasn't much of a question and sounded more of a statement.

"I've been waiting over ten minutes." Her hands rubbed her arms.

"Let me warm you." Daniel put his arm around her waist and pulled her closer. That's when he noticed her earrings. The earrings, as well as the dress, were new. He had opened an account with Saks for her, and he figured a bill would cross his desk soon.

Brandelynn's gaze caught his. Her eyebrow arched, and she stared at him like a tigress stalking prey. "You look handsome." She nearly sat on his lap and kissed him back.

The kiss was eager and welcomed, but it kept them from talking. The conversations they had never went much further than this. He wanted to either break up with Brandelynn or completely let her into his world, he wasn't sure which.

Whichever it was, this was an important decision and he needed to know more about her.

Her hand slipped into his suit pants and gripped his already hardened cock. He pulled away and thought back to the article and to what Evan had said.

He then asked, "Where did you grow up?"

5

*W*hy did women talk in riddles? A straight answer was all Daniel wanted, not a bunch of suspicious questions asking him what was wrong and why he was questing her like a criminal.

The article clearly stated that women wanted to talk about their lives and their feelings. What was he doing wrong?

He would check in with Evan—who seemed like the 'woman whisperer'—but Brandelynn had closed their privacy screen and blocked all sight and sound. The ride to the restaurant was short. If not, Daniel knew what the closed privacy screen usually meant.

And even though a quick romp in the car always felt good in the past, he just wasn't in the mood.

The car turned into the crowded parking lot of

Mas Rafs. People who had not planned ahead for reservations crowded the five–star restaurant.

Evan parked the car in front of the place, and walked to the rear door. He stood with his back to the car, giving them a moment of privacy.

Brandelynn touched up her hair and makeup. She was like an old gunslinger—fastest draw in the west, only with a compact. Daniel hadn't even noticed her remove the makeup from her purse.

He waited a few minutes while she made herself perfect. Now taking a good look at her, she almost seemed too perfect—nearly plastic. Blonde hair, thin waist, big boobs… She was Barbie personified.

She placed the compact back in her purse, and her cell phone fell. Picking it up, he noticed a text from, *"Black Cat."* He wasn't sure what *"Black Cat"* was, but they had a margarita special going on tonight. Brandelynn had never mentioned the place before, but maybe it was her hangout when she went out with her friends.

Friends he didn't know, and had never met.

"Thank you." She grabbed the phone from him and placed it into her purse.

Daniel tapped on the car window and Evan opened the door so the two could step out. Brandelynn hooked her arm around Daniel's outstretched one once they stood on the curb.

"Enjoy your meal, sir. Madam." Evan closed the car door. "I'll be right here when you need me, sir."

The young man hadn't said two words since getting into the car with Brandelynn. Daniel had asked for the truth, and the truth is what he got.

Evan took out his card and handed it to Daniel. "I'll park down the street. Just call when you're ready, sir."

Gone was Evan's happy expression and joy in doing his job. His expressionless face held his shame. Shame for only telling the truth.

Daniel felt like he should have said something to the boy, but instead, he took the card and let him drive away without a word.

Brandelynn fussed with her hair and waited, a scowl crossing her face. She was either a child who needed full attention, or a high maintenance woman who would rather be anywhere else. Either way, he hated that expression—and had seen it too many time in the past.

"We can go somewhere else if you want." Since Mas Rafs was his favorite restaurant, he hoped she would not suggest another place.

Her eyes widened. "This place is excellent. I assumed we'd be here tonight, seeing how we always come here."

He didn't appreciate the tone of her voice, but dismissed it.

Brandelynn's hand caressed her hair, her fingers picking up loose strands and she smiled toward someone taking her picture. Daniel suspected she liked the attention. Most of his past girlfriends enjoyed the fame, as if it was one of the perks of dating him.

He, however, could do without the paparazzi.

They passed the crowd, and he held the restaurant door for Brandelynn. All Daniel could think about was Evan back in the car, eating his sack dinner lovingly handmade by his wife. Daniel would quickly toss Mas Rafs aside if he had someone to make him a sandwich and wish him a good day at work. Did Evan even realize how lucky he was to have a banana split woman in his life?

"Mr. Ellington. Miss Brandelynn. So nice to see you again," Adam Levinson, the owner of the restaurant and a close friend of Daniel's, said once they made their way through the door.

"You have the best accommodation tonight, in our wine cellar room." Adam shook Daniel's hand with a firm grip. "There are three semi–private tables in the room, each partitioned off and staffed with their own wait staff."

Noting the way Brandelynn hugged his arm, having two other couples in the room would ensure they actually ate dinner tonight instead of cutting it short and rushing back to his place to have sex.

It would give them a chance to talk.

God, what was he thinking? One magazine and he was all touchy, feeling.

He felt pathetic.

Sitting at their reserved table, he stared into Brandelynn's eyes. She was beautiful, sexy, great in bed… but also conceited and shallow. Perhaps he had set the bar too high. After all, he was already six months into this relationship. Most women didn't survive this long.

"Smile, sweetheart." She turned her head and extended her hand to take a selfy of the two of them. She then began texting, "Hashtag romance, hashtag Valentine's Day, hashtag monthiversary…"

He let her words fade into the distance. In this one–hundred–and–forty–character–or–less attention span of a world, when did six months become a long time? His parents had been blissfully married for over fifty years until his mother's recent death.

Brandelynn looked devilishly at him and winked. "Hashtag handsome, hashtag…." Her voice sounded sugary-sweet with each word of flattery—but she still kept texting and snap-chatting.

Would she bother to type hashtag rich or hashtag meal ticket? Probably not. It was implied by just saying hashtag Ellington. Too bad hashtag soul mate wouldn't make the list either.

Maybe he was too successful to find a soul mate. His parents met when his father was struggling financially and all he could offer was his love and devotion. His parents were probably not much better financially off than Evan and his wife.

Maybe that was when Daniel should have found

someone. But at the time, he'd been more interested in sleeping around than finding someone who wanted him, not just his wallet.

Damn. He had lost the opportunity, and he only had himself to blame.

The waiter approached the table with menus in hand. "Good evening sir, madam." He handed them the menus. "Happy Valentine's Day to the both of you. We are offering some lovely specials tonight, starting with …"

Daniel allowed the man's words to fade into the background. He would order the sirloin steak, his favorite, once again. Steak, mashed potatoes, asparagus, and a salad on the side. Solid food. Once the waiter left, he said, "Everything sounds so good this evening."

She stared at the menu and didn't glance up.

He felt like he was on an awkward first date. A first date that wasn't going well. "You never told me what your favorite food is. Do you have a favorite meal?"

She glanced up. "What?"

"Do you have a favorite food?"

She shook her head and continued to read the menu. "It all looks good, sweetheart."

How could he negotiate massive business agreements, own an internationally successful business, hold two degrees—one in English—and yet not be able to start a conversation with a woman he was sleeping with?

Daniel didn't start dating Brandelynn for her conversation abilities, but he'd thought surely she would at least answer a direct question.

"I thought the Alaskan salmon special sounded fantastic," he said, trying again. "I've never been to Alaska. One of my bucket list items is to see the Northern Lights."

Brandelynn gave a slight "Uh–huh" as she continued to read.

"Have you ever seen them?"

"Seen what? The lights?"

"Yes."

She shook her head. "I grew up down south," she said, nearly dismissively.

Her diction held no southern accent. "What part of the south?"

The look she gave him was one of irritation, like she didn't want to talk at all.

"I think I'll have the lobster special." She smiled and Daniel realized even her teeth were capped.

The one thing Daniel knew always worked with women was gifts. He unbuttoned his coat and tapped the inside breast pocket of his jacket, feeling the diamond tennis bracelet Ms. Baxter had bought for tonight. So why did he feel like *he* was being served up with a big red bow?

6

The warmth of her sister's house surrounded Deborah after a cold drive, giving her a sense of family harmony. She always felt at home at Sue's place—that is, if her husband were gone. Otherwise, Deborah played the part of a third wheel.

Tonight, it was only the two of them, delicious Chinese food, and a bottle of wine. It was perfect.

Deborah helped herself to more of the chicken with broccoli and Sue finished off the garlic shrimp dish. There had been no mention of Sue's husband during the meal, so Deborah ventured to ask, "Have you heard from…?"

"No," Sue cut her off in an irritated tone, one that was filled with worry. "Deployed in Iraq and doing something secret."

Loneliness laced her words in a poison-filled, I

don't care if he is off saving the world he needs to come home, type of way.

Message received.

They returned to the living room and sat down. Deborah folded her long legs under her as she placed a pillow on her lap to use as a makeshift table. She then took a sip of her wine, the start of her second glass of the evening.

She normally limited herself to just one glass. But it *was* her birthday, and it *was* Valentine's Day, so two drinks were not out of the question. And she had felt off all day after getting to work. The eeriness of having Caroline offer to set her up on a date had made her skin crawl. Having to fish a gift from the sorry-to-see-you-go slush pile of jewelry trinkets she kept on hand for Daniel's ex-loves had added to the odd feeling.

Deborah had been waiting to give Daniel's current love interest her parting gift for several months now. Who knew the present would end up being a Valentine's Day gift?

Sue's eyebrow rose and had a playful expression on her face. "Over the years, has Mr. Boss Man gotten fat?"

Deborah nearly spewed her wine. She figured the subject would come around to her boss soon enough, but she'd thought the topic might be held at bay at least until the cheesecake was done defrosting for dessert.

So much for a perfect evening.

"Mr. Ellington is not fat."

"Balding?" Sue gestured to her face. "Bad dental work?"

"Nothing," Deborah managed to say between a fit of laughter. "He's still as handsome as ever." Handsome, and totally off limits.

Why had she told Sue about her crush on the man all those years ago? It wasn't destined to go anywhere, and was something she had no intention of pursuing. Office romances never worked out, and she didn't need the heartache. Or the shame of when it imploded in her face.

"Handsome as in he looks good for his age?" Sue pressed. "Or handsome as in I am dying inside not having his arms around me?"

Deborah pulled out her phone and went to the bookmark she kept for the company's website. The home page showed a recent image of the man, a picture Deborah had taken when the company had first moved to Chicago nearly a year ago. Daniel stood outside their building by the company's logo. His strong jaw showed his confidence, his whimsical smile his more playful side. With the clear blue sky behind him, and the stance he had taken, he looked like Superman.

"You don't keep up with the securities industry, or anything in my life, do you?" she asked her sister.

Sue shook her head. "Just Josh."

A slight smile spread across her lips—which was always the case when her son was mentioned.

Deborah glanced down at her phone. "This is a recent picture of my Mr. Boss Man." Rarely did Daniel allow himself to be photographed for public exposure, and this was a fantastic picture of him. He looked devilishly handsome in his dark and three-piece suit. What was it about that powerful—I can take on the world—look in his eyes that turned her to jelly several times a day?

Deborah turned the phone and allowed her sister to see who Deborah believed to be the most perfect man on the planet.

Sue's mouth gaped open. "The touch of gray in his lush hairline suits him." She studied the picture. "He still has the most gorgeous blue eyes, still has broad shoulders, and still has no idea you even exist."

"Enough." Deborah took the phone and pocketed it. "Mr. Ellington is off–limits. Besides, he's only interested in women half our age. He didn't even remember today is my birthday."

"Not even a card?" Sue shook her head in a 'how do you put up with that behavior' type of way. "Unbelievable."

Deborah faked a carefree smile. "So? He forgot my birthday. Mr. Ellington employs me, which is more than enough. He's under no other obligation."

Sue eyed her sister, causing Deborah to wonder if she had food on her face.

"You do everything for this man, and have for over eighteen years. You would think he could at least remember your birthday. My god, you've spent nearly two decades of birthdays with the man."

A piece of chicken fell from Deborah's fork and hit her comfy sweatshirt, leaving a small brown stain. "I'm fine," she said, blotting at the mess with a napkin and hoping to get the topic off her boss. "It's not as if this is the first year he's forgotten."

"Exactly my point. He doesn't appreciate you, Didi."

Deborah smiled and felt some anxiety escaping from her body at the sound of her childhood nickname.

Sue set her plate on the coffee table and grabbed her wine glass. "You should find another job. One with a boss who doesn't depend on you for everything. The man may be Greek God material, but there's no reason for him to not see you." Sue waved her hand out in the air between the two of them. "With your sexy brunette hair, sexy doe–like eyes, and sexy legs 'till Tuesday… I bet those girls he dates can't hold a candle to you."

Why did they have to talk about her boss every time they got together? Putting on her best don't–mess–with–me expression, Deborah said, "Nothing will ever happen between me and my boss. Besides, I enjoy my job." She set her plate down on the pillow in her lap. "The pay is fantastic. I wouldn't earn this type of money being anyone else's assistant."

"Have you tried looking around?"

"All the time," she said, knowing it was a lie. "But as usual, the deal I get from my current job is too good. Plus, it's great experience."

"You can do so much more." Sue pointed accusingly at her sister. "You almost have a college degree. You are one of the most intelligent women I know. And yet, you don't want to do anything more than be a glorified secretary?"

Deborah's chest tightened with the mention of the word secretary. She was so much more than that. Her sister needed to stop with her second glass of wine. By the third one, Sue usually plotted out what was wrong with the world and insisted how she knew how to fix everything.

"I'm not a glorified secretary." Deborah hated being called that. "You know I enjoy my writing."

Sue rolled her eyes. "You enjoy your little hobby."

It was a punch to the gut. No one understood how important writing was to her.

"I just self–published my second romance novel." Deborah held her chin high and took pride in her hard work. "The book is doing well, by the way."

"Did you sell more than five copies this time?"

The feeling of needles prickled up her spine and

she sucked in a deep breath before her ribs crushed in on her.

This was it. No more wine for her sister. Deborah could easily tear into Sue's life. The woman didn't have children, although that was because her husband couldn't have any. She hated her job, which, Deborah guessed most people did. Sue also lived in the smallest house in a nice neighborhood, but was heavily in debt.

Just as she was about to let loose on her sister, she saw Josh's picture hanging on the wall.

She owed Sue so much.

And even thought Deborah was unmarried, she had so much in her life because of her son. He had been the blessing in disguise that filled her life. A child that her sister would never have.

Deborah took a deep breath and then counted off on her fingers. "My pay is twice that of other assistants. My end of the year bonus check is fantastic. I get eight weeks off a year when Mr. Ellington vacations—and that doesn't include the holidays. And, Josh was awarded the Ellington–Weston scholarship—which is only granted to employees and their families. Since it's a four–year scholarship, I know I'm not going anywhere for at least that long."

Sue let out a deep breath. "How is my favorite nephew doing?"

A beam of pride crossed Deborah's face. Finally, a topic she could dive into. "He loved his first semester. He received all As on his report card."

"I miss him, Didi. Do you think he'll be around for spring break?"

Deborah relaxed more into the plush couch, thankful for the top change. "Maybe. This summer he'll work at Ellington–Weston again, which is nice. I think having interned there the last two summers helped him get into Texas Tech. Big universities like hard work and student diversity."

Sue sipped her wine. "Now that you're an empty–nester, and don't have to worry about raising a kid on your own, you should start dating again. Hell, maybe try marriage for once. You might like it."

Deborah shuddered as the discussion once again focused on what was wrong with her life. Her job was always the first target, and then her lack of a man. Why did her sister always want her to be dating someone? She should have realized dinner came with a side order of a life lecture. This was exactly why she only saw her sister every two months or so.

"My friend Caroline wants to set me up with someone. Since Josh is out of the house... perhaps I'll consider it," Deborah said, lying to appease Sue.

"You should." Sue waved her hand through the air. "You're beautiful, just like your sister. You work out every day and have a fantastic body that most twenty–year–olds would be jealous of. Your hairstyle is outdated, but…"

Deborah gently touched her long hair, which was collected in a ponytail. "I might take Caroline up on the offer. I don't know."

Sue grabbed the wine bottle and filled up her glass again.

How many drinks did that make it?

Too many.

Sue held the wine up and gestured for her sister to take it, but Deborah shook her head. She needed to drive home tonight, and let's face it, not *everybody* could be the family lush.

"Your friend won't find anyone more suited to you than your boss," Sue said. "You're with the man every day anyway. You take care of his office, you take care of his home… you should totally take care of him in his bedroom."

Wine made her sister bold, and forgetful. "You know exactly why I can never date Mr. Ellington."

Sue made a dismissive sound from the back of her throat. "You should have been dating the last twenty years. You let your twenties and thirties slip away."

"My twenties and thirties were spent raising my son." She leaned in, ready to count all the non-children that filled her sister's home.

Sue's finger shot up. "One mistake. You have punished yourself for years over one tiny mistake. To make things worse, you've surrounded yourself with reminders of it."

Deborah's jaw tightened as the shame of that fateful night once again flooded her thoughts. "Josh was not a mistake."

"No. The mistake would be his father."

7

*T*he evening wasn't going well, and the other couples in the semi–private Mas Rafs's dining room stared at Daniel's table.

He hated this type of attention.

One too many questions, had been asked. He had not realizing that, "Where do you see us in five years?" would lead to such a heated argument—especially when he had said he didn't see them getting married.

He squirmed in his seat once more. He wasn't sure why he had stirred the conversation down this route on Valentine's Day, of all days, but he couldn't take back what he had said. "Brandelynn, please keep your voice down."

The look she gave him could have been a death ray pointed to his head.

"Here's another reason..." she said, her voice

prattling off the fourth reason why the two of them should get hitched.

Should. Not want to. Not need to. Not wish to. But *should*. He wondered if she could hear what she was saying and if it sounded as crazy to her as it did to him.

Daniel stole a glance at the two other couples in the room. The man from table one had proposed to his girlfriend a good twenty minutes ago. The screams of delight, the resilient 'yes' that had come immediately afterward…it killed the moods at the other two tables.

As the newly engaged couple remained ecstatic and cooed with delight, the man at the second table seemed nervous. Since Brandelynn currently rattled off the fifth reason why they should also be getting married, Daniel could understand the way the man at table two felt.

Clink, clink

The man at the second table tapped his wine glass with his knife.

All eyes darted toward him. It got Brandelynn to be quiet for a minute. That was until the man held up a ring, knelt, and proposed.

Fuck.

The air in the room felt stifling.

Everyone cheered again for the second time. The wait staff held plastered smiles on their faces as they whispered and glanced toward Daniel as if three was the magic number tonight.

Double fuck.

There wasn't going to be a hat-trick, especially since, not even five minutes ago for the whole room to hear, Brandelynn had called Daniel a selfish bastard. The crowd needed to read the room.

Daniel once again held up his wine glass, nodded to the second happy couple and said, "Congratulations." The two men now had happy fiancées, but Daniel wasn't going to cave.

"Everyone is getting married, except us. Brandelynn's body stiffened and she eyed him like prey.

"You're a shallow miser." Brandelynn launched into the sixth reason the two of them should be married, her piercing voice cold and calculating, her face pinching into an evil witch-like appearance.

Daniel jaw tightened. He had always treated her well, treated her with respect, and treated her to many high-priced demands. As for being a miser, he had set up a college scholarship program for Ellington-Weston employees and their families. It was at his mother's request, but he had still done it. At this point, Brandelynn either really didn't know him, or she was just making shit up.

That's when he noticed that something was missing from her little tirade. How could she get to reason number six and not mention the word love?

He stared into her cold eyes and his body

shuddered like it had been hit by a blow from Jack Frost himself.

No 'I love you', 'I can't live without you', or even 'I need you in my life'. Nothing from the heart, only cold statistics of how long they've been dating and how most men propose by this time to their girlfriends.

Daniel knew in his heart that Brandelynn didn't love him. He was a meal ticket.

The beautiful green dress she wore, he had bought it. The diamond necklace around her neck, he had bought it. Even her breasts.... Well, you could argue that they were a gift to *him*. But, still. He had paid the bill.

In the candlelit room, he could make out the shine of the new highlights in her hair. Just like the way the dim light reflected off her new tennis bracelet.

She now pointed her finger at him to yell about reason number seven, and he held up his hand to stop her. He hadn't gotten to this point in life because he feared peer pressure. This was, or should be, a simple business transaction with two opposing parties.

"I'm not going to ask you to marry me because you're yelling at me to do so."

It was like he'd ignited a fuse.

He took a deep breath and sweat began beading on his forehead. Everyone stared in their direction. One held up a camera phone, but wasn't aiming it their way—not yet.

"Please lower your voice and listen." He leaned and half way covered his face to keep their conversation private. "We're not even dating exclusively, and you want to get married? We've only been together six months."

"Seven months."

Like that was a world of difference.

Had it really been seven months?

"And what do you mean, 'we're not even dating exclusively'?" Her crazy eyes zeroed in on him. "Are you dating someone else?"

He barely had time to date her, let alone another demanding woman. "We never discussed moving our relationship forward like that."

Her jaw locked and she crossed her arms in front of her. "I'm not going to wait around for you to decide if you want to marry me. Other men keep asking me out, and even if you weren't exclusive in this relationship, I always have been."

"I'm not dating anyone else." What was the point in trying to prove that to her when she was angry like this?

Her gaze softened, and she reached across the table to stroke his arm. His fingertips danced along the sleeve of his suit, and she played coy. "Things are going so well between us. I think that if we got married, we could spend more time together."

Her emotional roller coaster was a bit too bi-polar for him. And still, no mention of love.

Emptiness engulfed him—not because he wanted her, not because he needed her, not because he loved her—but because what he had suspected all along was true. She didn't love him past his wallet.

Even though it was Valentine's Day, it was time to let her go.

"I can't marry you, Brandelynn." The words slipped out, but they conveyed exactly the way he felt.

Her sweet, angelic, plastic face turned wild. Her body stiffened even more.

"Why can't you marry me?"

He thought for a second what to say that would somehow magically end this horrid evening. The idea of saying, *"Because I don't love you,"* came to mind. Knowing Brandelynn, she would argue her way out of that one and say that he didn't recognize he was in love with her. As if a man wouldn't know they were in love with someone.

"Because I'm already engaged," he blurted out.

Where the hell had that come from? The conversation with Scott and Ravi this morning must have really gotten under his skin.

Based on the look she gave him, he was thankful it was time for dessert, and the heavier knives had already been collected from the table.

"Who is she?"

He shook his head. "No one you know."

"Liar."

A flash of light caught his attention. He glared in the direction of the camera only to see that the waiter took a picture of the couple at table number two. Daniel took a deep breath, but his neck prickled, and the hairs on his nape stood on end. He didn't want to make a public display and have a front–page story featuring this breakup.

No crisis. No drama. No hassles.

"I'm not lying."

Brandelynn stared at him, her reddened face twisting her mouth into a scowl. "What's her name?"

"D…Didi… Didi Offutt." Where the hell had Didi come from? It was the first thing that'd popped into his mind.

"Didi? What is she? Twelve?" Her eyes narrowed at him as if she could tell the tale was a lie.

"For the last seven months, you've only ever been seen out with me. All those dinners at fancy restaurants, all those boring nights at the fucking opera, all those nights with you in bed… There hasn't been anyone else." She leaned in. "We fuck four nights a week, and always at your place. When do you even have time to see someone else, old man?"

Daniel twisted his napkin into a mess under the table. How dare she call him an "old man?"

"She's an heiress from Austria and has only recently come to town." He bit his lip once the words had escaped. Why an heiress? Why from frickin' Austria? This wasn't the Sound of Music.

"And you decided to marry her the second her plane landed?"

Why couldn't he just be a jerk and have Ms. Baxter break off his relationship with Brandelynn? His past women always got a parting gift, and it spared Daniel from seeing the women's tears when Ms. Baxter took care of the dirty work.

He was so bad at break ups.

But this engagement lie was a ticket out of another problem, and he was done cowing to Brandelynn and her ridiculous demands.

"My car will take you home. I'll take a cab." He stood and walked out of the semi–private dining room, feeling accomplished at his well thought out lie. What could possibly go wrong with it?

8

*D*eborah weaved her way through the crowded atrium in the Ellington–Weston building and got past security. More people wandered around the lobby today, which prickled the hairs on the back of her neck.

She heard reporters talking with their camera crew and could make out the names of local news stations on their huge cameras. Something was up this early in the morning.

Some anger bubbled up within her. The merger wouldn't be complete for another week, so that couldn't be it. It had to be that list. Are people that eager to disrupt the lives of others that they need something as frivolous as a top 10 man hunt list to preoccupy them?

Then, a glimmer of anxiety struck her. Maybe there had been an accident? There were certainly enough reporters here to cover anything. She scanned the lobby, trying to make out anything of interest but found nothing amiss. Figuring there would be police tape blocking her way if any danger existed, she pressed the elevator button and waited for the lift.

"Ma'am? Do you work for Ellington–Weston?"

Deborah caught a glimpse of a woman standing at the security section, trying to get her attention.

The reporter leaned on the gate and held up a microphone to get it as close to Deborah as possible. "I only need a moment of your time. I'd like to talk to you about Chicago's most eligible bachelor…"

Deborah couldn't put up with this for too much longer. She shook her head and turned away from the woman, not wanting to hear any more. Her phone had rung off the hook yesterday and all the reporters had wanted was a minute of her time.

One minute here, one minute there. Didn't people understand that she was busy? She had a job. She was a mother. If she gave everyone a moment of her time, she wouldn't have a minute in the day to use the bathroom.

She didn't even have time to drop off a package for Josh at the post office this morning.

"Do you work for Ellington–Weston?" The reporter held the mic higher and asked again as Deborah waited for the elevator. "We want to ask you questions about Daniel Ellington."

Deborah stared at the woman.

"How is Daniel Ellington feeling about this new development?" the reporter asked.

Daniel?

Deborah's heart raced as she dug her phone from her purse and turned her back to the reporter once again. Could something bad have happened?

No messages. She had listed herself as "Emergency Contact" in his address book. If something dire had happened, she surely would have been told.

Her gaze darted to the displays above each of the elevators. Why was it taking so long for one of them to come down?

The short elevator ride felt endless, letting off passengers one-by-one until Deborah finally stood alone. She took a deep breath once the bell dinged and the doors opened on her floor.

She was expecting to see a chaotic mess, but several people slowly milled about the area doing their regular routine, suggesting that nothing was wrong. Deborah took a deep breath, feeling a little relieved. Her security card swayed on a cord around her neck as she dashed past her co–workers and approached her office.

Once in, she tossed her coat on the chair next to her desk and took a seat. She logged in, and her computer came to life.

She first checked her email account. Nothing alarming jumped out at her so she scanned the company's SLACK and Skype feeds. She quickly studied the information, but the chatter appeared to be all business–related.

"Okay," she said to herself. "Just calm down. Everything seems in order."

The lack of anything out of the ordinary was a puzzle considering the zoo downstairs.

She opened her Tweet Dock account, which monitored the company's social profile and also any mention of Daniel Ellington.

The screen showed a column of notifications, messages, and activity, with the latter refreshing every few seconds. Messages streamed past, faster than she had ever seen them move before.

A weight plummeted in her stomach, nearly taking her to the floor as well. The trending hashtags of #offthemarket and #engaged were plastered on her computer screen next to the column monitoring Daniel's name.

She clicked a link and an online magazine called *Buzz News* popped up filled with ads, videos, and a barrage of color. Finally, she noticed Daniel's name. It was announcing his engagement.

Her heart felt heavy, and she could hardly breathe.

Deborah scanned the article, desperate for any signs that this was a joke. There was no picture of the betrothed, but the article held fast to its announcement.

Had Daniel asked his latest young girl–of–a–date to be his wife?

She glared at the calendar and counted back the time. Her eyes widened when she realized the two had been dating for seven months. Had they really been together that long?

Shit.

Deborah's stomach twisted, and a wave of nausea hit her. She'd known this day may come, especially since he was turning fifty soon. Daniel was one of the most eligible bachelors around. There really was no reason to feel queasy.

But she did. She felt very odd.

Deborah took some deep breaths. His fiancée, the woman Deborah had figured would be a flash in the pan, must be extraordinary to have landed such a fine man as Daniel.

She used the mouse to display more of the news, her hand trembling. According to the article, he was engaged to an Austrian heiress.

She bit her lip and pondered that thought. She had only met Daniel's flavor-of-the-month once, but had talked to her countless times on the phone and through text messages. The girl always came across as arrogant and self–righteous, which suggested she might come from wealth and feel entitled. Deborah just never thought of her as having any riches since the girl had a stereotypical personality of a trailer–park.

But if she were rich, the engagement did make sense. A billionaire like Daniel would never marry a commoner. He deserved to be in love and to find a good wife. There was nothing wrong with that.

After staring for a minute at her computer screen, and seeing the activity displayed on Tweet Dock race by, she grabbed her phone and texted Daniel to be on the lookout for the paparazzi in the lobby.

She had just set the phone down when it chirped, signaling that a text had come in.

It wasn't from Daniel.

"How was your birthday?"

At least it wasn't a nosy reporter. It was Caroline.

Deborah thought about typing, *"Lonely, depressing, and it ended with a bottle of wine and polishing off a fat–free cheesecake,"* but settled on texting a simple, *"Okay"* back.

Immediately, another text came from Caroline. This one asking for details.

Details?

Didn't the woman understand that it was a workday? Deborah was too busy to chat, and too upset to even think straight. She texted, *"Talk later?"* into the phone, but it buzzed again.

"Do you or don't you want me to set you up? I have a fantastic guy for you."

The mail needed to be sorted, coffee needed to be made, and the day needed to be started, but her knees felt weak. She wasn't sure she could even stand.

Deborah stared at her phone and knew Caroline waited for a reply.

After a few seconds, the words *"You there?"* came across the little screen.

Before she could change her mind, Deborah took a deep breath and texted. *"Fine. Set me up."* She then placed the phone in her pocket and told herself not to touch it again until lunchtime.

There was so much that needed to be done. Soon, the arrangements for the wedding would begin—gift registries filled out, a guest list created... a honeymoon to plan.

9

*D*aniel inhaled deeply, smelling the sweetness of the woman lying beside him and inviting the warmth of her body to caress him. His hands scooped her up, and he drew her closer, needing to bury himself within her. He felt the smoothness of her skin as her pert nipples pressed against his bare chest.

She giggled as she straddled his firm, bare form, opening herself up to him and the pleasure he would give her.

The sheets were filled with the fragrances of her perfume mixed with their passion and her moistened arousal. She arched her naked body, moaning for more.

He flipped her over, taking the more dominant position. He moved his hand up her inner thigh where the silkiness of her skin welcomed him. Her knees shifted upward, allowing him access to her most private parts.

His fingers slid down to find her glistening folds to stroke. She was wet and ready for him. He pushed his throbbing member into her, causing her breathing to become labored and she encouraged him to continue.

Her beautiful, brunette hair splayed across her face, only allowing her full, red lips to be visible to him as she panted. She bit down just as her hips bucked under him. He nearly brought her to the edge, but he paused.

He wanted to see her face.

He needed to know who lay in bed with him. He shifted his body to a better position where he could move her hair to see her face, but she placed her hands on his shoulders and pushed him down, suggesting that she wasn't quite finished.

He would claim her, but only after he had identified her. She moaned his name as he brushed her hair aside to finally reveal her face. He glanced down...

And was abruptly woken by his alarm clock.

His heart raced as he heard it play, *"Away at the Races"* loudly on the nightstand. He grabbed it in an attempt to silence it, but his dogs jumped on the bed and began licking his face, causing him to fumble with the snooze button.

"Good boy, good girl," he said, giving each one a

pat on the head once he stopped his alarm. Oreo nudged his arm and whined. Ginger barked. They needed to go outside, which meant he should get up.

He was *up* already. Firm and hard and making a tent out of the sheets.

The vivid dream had left him filled with desire and frustration, and now, smelly dog breath covered him. He sat up and allowed the blankets to fall. His sweaty aroused body instantly cooled in the air–conditioned room.

Dammit. That was the most erotic dream he had ever had. So life-like that he could swear his dream woman had been in bed right next to him. A curvy, beautiful… brunette.

Odd that he wasn't dreaming of Brandelynn, who was blonde.

He had dreamt of this same brunette last week too. Some mystery woman. Sexy, tantalizing, beautiful, unknown.

His heartbeats slowed as he took in more deep breaths. The magazine lay on the nightstand, and must have been the prompt for his subconscious mind to dream of such a fantasy woman. He had read the publication cover–to–cover and had to admit that some of the articles made a lot of sense. The second quiz alone was an eye–opener. According to the results, he wanted to find a mate who was trustworthy, independent, and caring.

Overall, pretty generic descriptions of a

significant other. The last question suggested the most important thing to Daniel was to have someone as an equal to share his life with.

He was the richest man in Chicago, and he didn't hire personal household staff because he valued his privacy too much. How the hell was he going to find his equal in this world?

He stared at the empty spot in the bed next to him. The magazine said that everyone has a match; you just had to be willing to search and never settle. He had settled for less his entire life. Under his breath, he swore he'd fill his bed, and his life, with the perfect dream woman.

That was it. Daniel had hit his limit, and he planned to build a virtual wall around himself. No one would get in.

"They were even at my house this morning." The anger of the blatant disregard of his privacy bubbled up from low in Daniel's bowel to settle in his throat. The valve of his temperament exploded, but instead of screaming, he slammed his fist on his office desk, tipping the coffee in his mug and causing a drop to spill.

Ms. Baxter pulled a tissue from a Kleenex box and quickly wiped up the liquid.

As he took his seat, the plush leather, high–back

chair let out a slight squeak. He unbuttoned his suit jacket, now realizing how hot and stifling the room felt. "Do you know how annoying it is to wake up to journalists camped outside your front gate?"

Deborah straightened the mail and miscellaneous paperwork on the desk into a neat pile. "My house doesn't have a front gate, but I can imagine."

Her tone wasn't exactly sarcastic, more chastising in a humbling way. And it grounded him once again to reality.

Taking a deep breath, he told himself that his first–world problems were not the end of the world, and that he was fine. He raked his hand through his hair and reminded himself that with power and prestige came status and stress.

"Now, aren't you glad you bought a home on the outskirts of the city, one with a security fence and a long, private driveway, instead of the condo downtown? Out of all the places I scouted out for you, I knew this house suited you the best and met all your security needs."

Ms. Baxter knew him so well.

She was the only person—other than his psychologist—that he had told the story of his abduction to. He had been six years old and at a crowded mall with his mother. His father had just landed a successful business deal and had come into a substantial sum of money—enough for a newspaper to write up an article about them that included a family picture. His mother had taken Daniel shopping for some nice clothes when a woman—one with crazy eyes—had come out of the shadows and grabbed him.

The mall had gone on immediate lockdown, and security caught her before she could exit the building with him, but not before she drugged him, changed his clothes, and cut his hair. He remembered none of it. Immediately after she'd grabbed him, his whole world had gone dark. It wasn't until he woke up later in the hospital and people told him stories that he even knew what had happened. But it still left a mark.

It was dangerous to be at the center of the public eye.

Anonymity was important, with only a few trusted people close to you.

Deborah's hand supportively touched the back of his. Her knowing smile reassuring and strong.

She could stay within his virtual security wall. Everyone else could go to hell.

He removed his jacket, and she took it from him and hung it on the hanger of the standing valet.

"Don't let these idiots ruin your day, Mr. Ellington. Perhaps, you may want to leave early and disrupt your routine. You can pick up your current lady friend and arrive home before the next group of people camp out."

He hadn't thought of Brandelynn since last night, and a pang of guilt ran through him. Whether or not she was his 'the one', he should have confirmed she got home. Made sure she was okay. He was certain that Evan was a stand-up guy though, and did his job.

Daniel had swung by the car after he'd left the restaurant to let Evan know about the change of plans. He also told him he was right in his assessment of Brandelynn. She was all wrong for him.

Ms. Baxter's hand brushed the back of the jacket, shaking any lint from it. "If you get home early enough, the press may not even get a picture of the two of you together."

Her voice was controlled and flat, not exactly the way she normally sounded. "A picture of Brandelynn and me? Whatever for?"

Ms. Baxter's hand smoothed the creases from the jacket and then buttoned the top button. "Your big evening last night, of course. You got engaged to Brandi... Brandelynn." Her voice cracked as she stumbled upon the name. She fiddled more with the jacket and smiled at him. "Congratulations."

He was never sure how rumors like this got started. He absolutely did not want to hitch his wagon to such a mess like Brandelynn. His hand waved dismissively toward her. "I'm not engaged to that woman. We broke up last night."

She staggered to the chair and sat. "If you're not marrying Brandelynn, whom are you marrying?"

Again her voice sounded distant, and this time her face had paled. It seemed like such an incredible lie at the time—one to keep all to himself—but with the puzzled look Ms. Baxter gave him, he had to tell her. "I made the engagement up."

Her mouth gaped open. "But, why would you do that?"

His muscles relaxed and his body gave into the plush leather of the chair. This was exactly what he didn't want. The night should have ended with him leaving the restaurant. Him unentangled from Brandelynn, him off the list, him back to his private sanctuary with Deborah just concentrating on more important matters.

He shared with her his concern about the Top 10 Bachelor list, how Brandelynn wasn't the woman for him, and how making up a fake fiancée seemed like a clear solution to both problems.

"Let me get this straight," Deborah said. "You don't want to be engaged, so you made up a fake engagement."

God, it sounded so stupid when she said it. Last night, with a few scotches in him, the lie had made perfect sense. He had to admit now though, it did seem a bit farfetched. Sharing the details felt a bit embarrassing, but he said, "I made up a woman named Didi and said she was a wealthy heiress."

"Your imaginary fiancée is named Didi?" Her voice rose—almost accusatory in tone—when she said the name

"Didi Offutt." When Ms. Baxter's face paled, he asked, "What?"

"Of all the names in the world, you used my childhood nickname and the city I grew up in as your pretend bride–to–be?"

It was like a veil lifted and he could think straight. Daniel took in a deep breath, thankful that he'd figured out the Didi name mystery. Why on earth would that name have occurred to him?

Of course. He had taken that stupid magazine quiz and it had asked about your partner's childhood. It had subconsciously been on the top of his mind the whole night. "It was the first name that popped into my head. I'm sorry."

"I told you that name years ago. I'm surprised you even remembered it." Her face hardened. She didn't look angry, just a bit hurt. "I'm glad my personal stories serve you so well."

He didn't need Ms. Baxter upset with him; he always did better when she stood by his side. Plus, it pained him to see her hurt. The look on her face right now tore into him. "I don't know why your name popped into my head," he said, not wanting to explain that he read such a silly magazine cover-to-cover. "But don't worry. I figured this would all blow over after the fifteen minutes of fame the reporters are giving it."

"Blow over?" She walked to her office and brought back her phone. She punched in a few buttons. "Watch this."

His gaze went to the top left of the screen, and he

saw the words Tweet Dock. He didn't like social media, but he understood the power of it.

The middle column kept refreshing, with new tweets coming in containing his name with a hashtag. His knees turned to rubber, and he knew his whole world had changed. The lie hadn't even begun twenty-four hours ago and it looked like Armageddon. "Shit." He looked at Ms. Baxter. "Are you telling me I'm trending?"

"Of course, sir. Big news like this and you're the talk of the town." She slid the phone into her pocket. "They won't be satisfied until they have all the details."

"Details?" Details meant personal information. The release of which left you vulnerable. A queasiness grew in his belly, enough to make him sick. "There are no details. I'm engaged so I'm off the list."

"Doubtful unless there's follow-up data to support the engagement. Plus, you just invited every reporter in town who would want to cover your engagement and marriage to come hunt you down." She counted off on her fingers. "The press will want a confirmed wedding date, a picture of the expensive ring, a confirmation of venue options. They'll want to know her background, and, of course, they'll want a picture of the two of you together."

Shit.

His chest tightened and he loosened his tie. He

had always been good tying up loose ends, but not made up ones. They weren't tangible enough for him to see, not that he even cared to be on the lookout for them.

Plus, he didn't want this type of exposure. He was too busy for this. His company's newest release was due out, he was in the middle of negotiations for a new business venture, the merger... "I'll say the engagement was called off."

"You could. But then the press could find out about the truth and write that you're a liar, or worse, they may believe you and want to dig into the reason the wedding was canceled."

And then, he'd still be on that damn bachelor list. This entire nightmare needed to go away, but he knew it'd exist until the list was printed. Scott said the official list would be out a couple of weeks from Valentine's Day.

Damn it. That meant at least two solid weeks of sheer torture.

The room felt as if it were growing smaller. Press would be everywhere. There'd be crowds of people everywhere Daniel went. People who didn't just want the latest news but may also want to hurt him.

God. Should he hire a bodyguard? He'd have to get recommendations, conduct interviews,...by the time he hired the right, trustworthy person the list would already be out.

He glanced at Ms. Baxter. She always took care of

the mundane details. Maybe things wouldn't escalate so quickly if they were handled properly, and if he could trust anybody it'd be her. "Perhaps you can smooth things over with the press."

A pause settled in between them, as though neither one knew what 'smooth things' over could really entail. "Maybe just run interference. Have me always in meetings or conferences whenever someone calls."

"Of course, sir. I don't know what I can do, but I'll help any way I can." She looked at her watch. "Your ten o'clock appointment will be here shortly." She stood and crossed the floor. "I'll escort him to the conference room once he arrives."

There wasn't much time, and Daniel's head spun with possibilities of how Deborah could solve all his fake engagement problems. One solution stuck in his head, but to accomplish it, he needed his lawyer. Picking up the phone, he called Scott.

10

*D*eborah's phone buzzed. Once again, it was a number she didn't recognize so she ignored it. That made five calls today so far, and it was only lunchtime.

She didn't have time for foolish fantasies of pretend engagements. Talking to the press? This was no doubt the weirdest thing she had ever been asked to do. The press calling her company phone was already a problem. She never liked lying to people, but this felt different. All of the lies she tells to the press would be printed.

Yikes.

She'd have to be careful.

Maybe she could just say 'no comment' all the time, not answer her phone, or…maybe it was time to take a short holiday away from the office.

She chuckled inside. A vacation right now would

really mess up Daniel's plans. No, she couldn't do that to him, not when he needed her now more than ever. She wasn't sure what she was going to do to 'run interference', but she'd have to worry about that later.

She checked her to–do list while she dashed from one errand to the next during her lunch break, thankful she now wore sneakers and not the high heel monstrosities. Her toes ached and reminded her that she needed to no longer buy pointy-toed shoes, even if they look fantastic and posh.

She studied the to-do list. Car repairs. Dry Cleaning. Buying deck furniture.

Check. Check. Check.

Yep. Everything for Mr. Ellington was taken care of. Although, she wasn't sure why he all of a sudden wanted new deck furniture. The wrought-iron set she had purchased for the home still looked great, and had very little wear.

A text came in from Daniel, and the *Hail to the Chief* sound-bite she had set for him played.

Deborah took a deep breath. As much as she loved being the one to swoop in and save the day, she wasn't sure how she could help him now. Running errands at lunch had felt like some semblance of a normal day, but she knew it'd be chaotic again once she returned to the office.

She read the text. "*Reschedule 1 pm meeting for later today*."

She read the text a second time. He needed her help with something business-related, not personal. That was good. That was regular routine and mundane. But, didn't he understand that she had already rescheduled that meeting twice with the CTO?

Shit.

At the very least, Deborah could cancel the current appointment on her cell phone. She'd have to reschedule when she was back in the office, but she wasn't looking forward to talking to the CTO's assistant and looking like an idiot asking for another timeslot.

Why did Daniel want to cancel his one o'clock meeting anyway?

Actually, she knew why. Daniel hadn't acted this way in years, but after breakups he tended to fall back into his adolescent routines. She just didn't want to think about what he might be doing in his office right now. It also explained the emergency need for deck furniture. Brandelynn may be gone, thank goodness, but that didn't mean another floozy wasn't comforting him.

Her body stiffened, and she momentarily closed her eyes. She had been dismissed like a younger sister being told to go to the movies. The situation was appalling and humiliating, but did it have to be dismissive as well?

She took a deep breath and told herself that it was

none of her business who else was making her boss feel better. She just hoped that the stewardess from his last flight, the waitress from the restaurant he last ate ate—or whomever the woman may be—was gone by the time she returned to the office.

Bumping into a young, very stupid girl on her way out the door—buttoning her blouse, her hair tussled—was always embarrassing. His couch escapades were nearly legendary in his twenties, they subsided a bit in his early thirties, now, nearly forty (as few as they were), they were beneath him. In so many ways he had matured, taken on so much responsibility, so much refinement…and yet in other ways, he was just a boy.

God, why did she love him so?

He never paid her a moment's notice. Of course, she wasn't batting her eyelashes at him and wearing see-through blouses to get his attention.

Daniel's women were all the same. They either suffered from daddy issues or had a huge craving for Mr. Ellington's fat wallet.

Shallow, insensitive, sexy.

A jealous rage continued to grow inside her, but then the Bible–thumping lectures of her parents replayed in her mind and the line between moral and immoral was again painted in front of her.

Bosses were off limits, even ones with melt-your-knees blue eyes, deep take-me-now voices, and firm six-pack-and-then-some abs.

He had even aged well with a light touch of gray at the hairline.

Daniel never saw his exes after the breakups, which was one of the many reasons she never considered him a fish to hook from the company pier. Nothing good would come of a relationship. She needed her job too much to take such a risk.

Daniel didn't have much time, and everything had to go like clockwork.

He entered his office and was happy that Ms. Baxter remained out to lunch.

His quick stop at the bank to retrieve an item from a safety deposit box hadn't taken long. It was an errand he would have normally dispatched Ms. Baxter for, but it was too delicate in nature.

He placed the small item in his desk drawer and heard the familiar voice of his lawyer as he knocked on the door and said hello.

Scott paused long enough to hang up his coat before he joined Daniel in his office and closed the door.

"The paperwork is all here." Scott handed Daniel an envelope. He let out a slight chuckle. "I still can't believe you asked me to write this up. You're lucky I had a light schedule this morning."

"Thanks for drafting it so quickly." He slid the

paper out, and the two sat down. "I know it was an odd request."

"I left the intended bride's name as a blank field, just in case Ms. Baxter doesn't agree and you need to find another fiancée." When Daniel nodded, Scott added, "Why did you suggest Ms. Baxter as the party of the second part when you could hire an actress and have her sign the nondisclosure?"

Daniel thought about that. Ms. Baxter always stood by his side and seemed to be the perfect choice. She was poised and educated, a quality woman.

An image of a banana split entered his mind.

She was definitely a banana split.

Plus, she was the one who'd told him this lie wouldn't just blow over without details. Ms. Baxter was the most detail–oriented person he knew.

And, it felt right.

"Ms. Baxter is loyal and dedicated. One of the few individuals in this world I can trust." He then added, "She'd never let something like this get to her head, either. Any other woman might get the idea that I was falling for them and that she could somehow turn this into a real engagement."

"Is trust the only reason?" Scott asked.

Daniel glanced across the desk. Trust was a big part of his life, and he only let a few people in his inner circle. Next to love, trust was the most important thing. "I trust Ms. Baxter with my home, my bank accounts…even my dogs. I won't have to worry if she agrees to do this."

"I see," Scott said, nodding. "The two of you aren't…" he let his question trail off and lifted an eyebrow suggestively.

"What? No." Did no one understand that a no-dating policy when it came to employees definitely included personal assistants? "Of course not."

Scott glanced at the paperwork. "I wrote the contract assuming not, but let's be honest, Deborah has been at your side for decades. If there had every been any feelings, any physical or…" He let out a deep sigh. "This is really delicate, and emotions run high when a ring is involved. As your legal counsel, I need to know. Are you currently, or in the past have you ever slept with Ms. Baxter?" Before Daniel could answer, he added, "And I'm talking sexual intercourse in any form."

The man may be a close friend, but this was downright prying into his personal life, and Daniel didn't like it. Still, he answered, "I have never had sex with her. I'm not sleeping with her now, and I don't plan to sleep with her any time in the near future." His voice rose in volume with each statement so he quickly glanced at the shut door that led to her office. She was still out to lunch thanks to his last minute, 'please buy me deck furniture request' and couldn't have heard him.

Scott raised his hands in surrender. "I just need to

have full disclosure so I know how to legally protect you and your interests if any issues arise."

Daniel hated revealing private matters to people. "I'm not interested in Ms. Baxter." Deborah may be his *office wife*, but there could never be anything else between them. "She's like a sister. You know…she knows how I like my coffee, she runs all my household errands, keeps my schedule running smoothly…"

"I have a sister, Daniel. She doesn't do any of that for me."

A grin appeared on Daniel's face. "Sounds like you need to train your sister better."

It was a joke, but judging by Scott's expression, he didn't think it was very funny. Daniel took a deep breath and picked up the contract once again. "I selected Deborah because I trust her."

"Well, all right then. You did just break up with Brandelynn so I just wanted to make sure it wasn't because of Deborah."

Closing his eyes, Daniel took a deep breath and counted to ten. The silence engulfed them, and then he finally said, "I broke up with Brandelynn because I didn't love her. My dream woman isn't Deborah…" He then thought about the woman who had featured heavily in his dream last night.

Hot. Sexy. Curly-haired brunette. Her curves were etched in his memory. Who was she?

"Dream woman?" Scott asked.

"I don't even fantasize about the Deborah, even though she's been at my side for years."

"So… you're not interested in her. Understood."

Daniel wasn't sure why he wanted to share—maybe it was due to the intimate nature of their discussion—but he said, "I dreamt of a beautiful brunette a few days ago and again last night. A sexy and alluring woman that…" He shook his head. "She's a mystery woman. I feel that she's out there somewhere. A total stranger now but someone I want to find." The truth sounded silly, but he needed Scott to understand that he didn't fantasize about Deborah. If anything, he fantasized about his dream woman—and hoped each night he'd see her in his dreams again.

"You're dreaming of a brunette?" Scott's eyebrow rose and Daniel knew the next remark would be snarky at best. He didn't need to be the butt of any jokes. "Is this the same brunette from a dream last Thanksgiving?" Scott then shook his head. "The same woman from a dream during Christmas?"

A tingling sensation engulfed Daniel. There had been other dreams, and he had told Scott briefly about them. "Forget I said anything." Why did he even mention it? No one needed to know his fantasies.

"Who is it? Not a new hire, right?" His face showed concern in a 'we won't have a sexual harassment suit on our hands' kind of way.

Daniel let out a deep sigh. "I never see her face in the dreams, so I have no idea who she is."

Scott let out a slight chuckle. "A sexy, dream brunette…I doubt a vision of your subconscious could sue you, so that should be safe." Scott cleared his throat and gazed down at the paperwork. "Anyway, this document includes a standard nondisclosure agreement. So, for the next two weeks, Deborah will act as your fiancée, in name only. She can't tell anyone about the arrangement. There is a clause about what would be appropriate for public displays of affection and what is off–limits."

Displays of affection? Daniel hadn't thought about…he read the indicated paragraph and mentally checked it off. "Kissing, hugging…gazing into each other's eyes, hand–holding…," Daniel read aloud. The affection was all middle school level, nothing too explicit—nothing too explosive if anything went wrong. "This is all acceptable."

Daniel then remembered something. "Ms. Baxter mentioned stuff like leaking a date to the press, a honeymoon destination, and other bridal things." Daniel felt the pressure building from a list of details he couldn't care less about. "I don't want to have to hire a fake wedding coordinator, as well."

Scott gave an all-knowing nod. As a recently married man, Daniel figured he could understand the headaches.

"I doubt it will come to that," Scott said. "But we

could do a fake bachelor party. I know Ravi would be on board. We could go to Atlantic City, or even hire party girls."

The suggestion would have been fine coming from Ravi, but hearing Scott say those words just sounded off. "Party girls? You're blissfully married. What do you know about 'party girls'?"

"Nothing. But my bachelor party, which you had to miss, was hosted by Black Cat."

"Black Cat?" Daniel perked up at the name. He figured it was a bar of some sort, not a gentlemen's club. It had been on his list of things to Google, but he had been too busy.

"It's an upscale strip place downtown. Why?"

A strip club? Well, that piece of information saved him from having to run an internet search on it. Daniel thought back to the car ride last night and the text Brandelynn had received. "I guess you'd have to be a regular customer to get the club to text you their specials."

"Push notifications?" Scott asked.

Daniel didn't know, and didn't care what they were called. Brandelynn received a text last night from Black Cat, so she must frequent the place, but that was odd since men were the clientele. "It doesn't matter," he said, shaking his head and brushing it off.

He stared at the document in his hands, and a sentence caught his attention that threatened to give him a powerful migraine. "The contract says that if she is an employee of Ellington–Weston that she'll be allowed time off between now and the end of this agreement. I can't go without an assistant that long."

Scott's expression changed as though he knew this would be a sticking point. "Do you want Deborah as your fiancée, or as your employee? You can't have it both ways."

The man had a point, but that didn't help the sick feeling brewing in the pit of Daniel's stomach.

"You can hire a temp to help out." Scott pointed at a section written lower on the page. "During the time off, Deborah can stay in a suite at the Langtham Hotel."

"Langtham? That's rather fancy, don't you think?" It was one of the oldest and most distinguished hotels in Chicago. He bet Trump even stayed there at times, even though the man owned Trump Tower.

Scott shrugged. "The media is reporting that she's an Austrian heiress. Naturally, we'll keep the location under wraps, but if the press finds out where she's staying, it has to be believable."

That did make sense. And, overall, the cost was negligible.

Flipping to the next page, Daniel noticed a wardrobe budget and a list of dates. "You have us going out to dinners, and to the opera." He loved the opera, but…a grunt escaped the back of his throat. "I don't have a lot of time. Business is keeping me working all hours of the day."

When Scott didn't flinch or concede the point, Daniel knew that he wouldn't be able to escape the nights out. "I'll get Ms. Baxter to make these arrangements."

"No need. Caroline came up with these suggestions and already booked everything, including spa treatments while Deborah stays at the hotel."

His inner safety wall was crumbling. Secret affairs needed to remain just that—secret. "Caroline knows about this?" Daniel set the paper down and glared at Scott.

"You said I could use a trusted consultant if needed. Believe me, I trust my wife. If it hadn't been for her help, I wouldn't have been able to come up with any romantic dates where you could parade your fake fiancée."

The defensive wall he erected slowly came down. "I guess that's all right." Daniel rubbed his jaw and placed the contract on the desk. "If Ms. Baxter does agree to do me this favor, she can discuss things with Caroline. The two of them are friends, and Ms. Baxter may need help if she is to be sequestered for two weeks at a hotel."

Daniel let out a deep sigh. Two weeks. God, he was asking a lot of her. "I just need to talk with Ms. Baxter and get her to sign on the dotted line."

"And, Daniel, if she's going to be your fiancée, you might want to stop calling her 'Ms. Baxter.'"

11

*D*eborah exited the elevator—painful, yet stylish, shoes back on her feet squishing her sensitive and sore toes—and made her way to her office. She opened the door and was grateful that she had a minute to put away her purse and comfy shoes before Mr. Ellington...

Wait.

Her gaze shifted and her head spun toward Ellington's private office.

She had been right. His door was closed. Unless he had a meeting, and she knew he didn't, he preferred to keep his office door open—always complaining that the air became stagnant in the room since he couldn't open the windows.

Her body stiffened. She opened the drawer to her desk and tossed her purse in. Next, she struggled with her coat, turning the sleeves inside-out in her haste.

She threw the coat on top of her desk. Who would it be this time? A sexy flight attendant? A sexy grease–monkey? A sexy college grad?

Mr. Ellington's breakup remorse usually had him going through a series of affairs.

It wouldn't be the first time a giggly young woman left Mr. Ellington's office, panties in hand, as Mr. Ellington asked Deborah to escort her out of the building. He'd promise to call the afternoon delight soon, but Deborah knew better.

She was always the clean-up crew for his romances.

What Mr. Ellington needed was a good woman to settle down with. He was more of a lonely man than a hound dog lusting for women. Why couldn't men see what they needed in life?

Deborah sat in her chair and sifted through some paperwork, not paying attention to the documents since her gaze wandered to the closed door every few seconds. Thankfully, she couldn't hear anything—this time.

The door opened, and Mr. Scott Hollister shook hands with Mr. Ellington before they left the office and entered hers.

She looked toward the coat rack. A man's jacket hung there.

Letting out a deep breath, she stood and walked to the rack, feeling foolish for not noticing the coat before.

"Do we need to schedule any appointments?" she asked the men, her voice slightly higher than she had intended.

Scott took his jacket from her. "We're good."

"Please say hello to Caroline for me, Mr. Hollister."

"I will, thanks."

Deborah opened the office door and let him out. Focusing now on Mr. Ellington, she said, "I've rescheduled the meeting with the CTO for three o'clock today."

"Deborah, I'd like to see you for a moment," Mr. Ellington said as she made her way back to her desk.

She stopped mid stride. He never called her "Deborah."

Deborah followed Mr. Ellington into his office where he immediately gestured for her to take one of the two seats in front of his large, and intimidating, office desk.

She crossed her legs and her foot began to shake. In an effort to stop the nervous twitch, she straightened her pencil skirt and placed a hand on her knee.

Something was off. She handled Mr. Ellington's schedule and there was no meeting with Scott for this afternoon. No. Their meeting had to be spur of the moment, with Daniel calling his lawyer in for a private pow-wow.

"Would you like a drink?" Daniel waved his hand and motioned to his mini bar in the corner of the room. His face softened and a huge smile graced his lips. "It's after lunch. Would you care for a sherry, scotch…?" He walked to the bar and glanced down as if taking inventory of the beverage selection.

There was no need to recite a menu. She kept his bar stocked.

"Perhaps a glass of wine?" he asked.

That was it. He was going to dismiss her. No matter what the government said about employment rates getting better, layoffs were occurring all over the city. She should have seen this coming.

She felt a lump in her throat, a heavy one that made it hard to breathe. "I don't drink, Mr. Ellington. But water would be nice."

He picked up the bottle of scotch. "Do you mind if I enjoy something a little stronger?"

"Of course not, sir."

Her heart raced as he poured himself a drink, the glass of the bottle clinking against the tumbler. He then sat back down and handed her a chilled bottle of water.

She felt the cool wetness of the bottle against her palm as she opened the container and took a sip. A drop of condensation dripped to her skirt, and she brushed it away.

Closing the bottle, she realized she had no coaster so she held on to it, playing with the label.

Whatever this was about, she needed to make everything right. Her son Josh needed the company's scholarship, otherwise...well, she'd have to find a job that paid more money. *A lot* more money.

And with a new job she would need to learn a new routine with limited vacation days. Any possibility of writing, except maybe on weekends, would be lost.

A frenzied chill shot through her. She didn't want to leave this job. She loved coming to work here.

"Here you go." Daniel tossed her a coaster for her water.

A man who actually cared about the furniture and knew how to use a coaster?

She was going to miss Daniel. There had never been so much as even a flirtatious smile between the two of them, but, on some level, he was her *work husband*.

A tear threatened to escape, but she held it back.

She didn't need a man in her life. Taking care of Daniel's routine, his house...his little puppies.

Her face pinched, and she told herself not to cry. She really loved those puppies. She had helped him pick them out and gave them their names.

She needed to focus on work and this moment. She'd have to clear out her desk, then she'd likely be escorted from the building—as though no longer trusted by anyone. And she'd have to return the office and house keys. Daniel was only her boss. She could find another job.

"How long have you been with the company?"

Her heart jumped and settled in her throat. "Nearly twenty years, sir," she said, her voice cracking. He knew how long she had been with Ellington-Weston. This was just small talk to lighten the blow.

He only nodded slowly. A nod that elevated her worry level from yellow to red and then to purple.

"You started as my father's secretary, right?"

She knew she was an older assistant. Maybe not as youthful and pretty as some of the younger women these days, but she had experience. That should count for something.

Actually, it should count for everything, but this was still a man's world.

"I worked for your father for nearly a year. Back when the company struggled with venture capitalist funding."

His nodding quickened. "I remember those days. So long ago."

She didn't want to remanence down memory lane. If only he'd get to the point. "Mr. Ellington, before you continue...."

"How is your son doing in college?"

The sinking feeling in the pit of her stomach hit rock bottom.

Mr. Ellington had approved Josh's scholarship

application. Secretly, she believed he'd chosen her son not only because Josh had interned for the company but also because of who he was. If Daniel were bringing the topic of Josh up, she must be losing her job as well as his scholarship.

"Josh is doing well," Her voice sounded shaky, so she steeled her resolve and firmly said, "He is studying hard, and the Ellington–Weston scholarship is going to good use."

The smile on his face didn't reassure her.

"He's a good kid," Daniel said with what she believed to be genuine sincerity. "With a good work ethic. Many people around here like him."

A blush came across her face. Josh had picked up the office routine quickly as an intern and had made some good friends around the office. "He's a good boy." She then corrected herself. "A fine young man."

His hand fidgeted with a document on his desk. The papers were turned over, and she assumed it was a separation agreement. She now understood why his lawyer had been here this morning without a scheduled appointment. How much severance did a person get after nearly two decades of loyal work? Two weeks? Maybe a month?

A bead of sweat formed on her brow so she wiped the moisture away. She had done nothing wrong. At least, nothing she could think of to risk her career with the company. She shouldn't criticize herself for getting caught up in a layoff. Things like this happened all the time.

But then again, if Scott needed to personally take care of the separation agreement... She felt a heaviness in her chest, and it became difficult to breathe. She was probably being dismissed as both Daniel's work and personal assistant. Simply wiped from his life like she never existed. This felt more severe than she could ever have imagined. Why, all of a sudden, would...And then a sinking feeling overcame her. Had Mr. Ellington found out about the incident?

Not able to make eye contact with her boss, she shifted in her seat. It had been years since that one indiscretion. No one knew about it.

Total secret.

One mistake.

She bit her tongue. No, Josh was never a mistake. Only his father was.

Maybe she should take that drink now.

Pretending to ask someone to marry you was much harder than Daniel realized. His hands were sweaty and staining the paper he held.

A silent pause filled the office, and he didn't know how to continue. Breaking the ice by talking about Deborah's son seemed only to make everything more awkward. Deborah wasn't even making eye contact with him anymore.

She'd been pregnant when he first met her, and he assumed divorced before Josh was even born. He had never heard her mention the father again, or, for that matter, another man in her life. She worked hard, raised her child alone, and did an excellent job with both.

He never thought of her dating. Never thought of her as being in a relationship. Never—well, rarely—allowed himself to think of her as a woman.

She was just a mother juggling a career. A mother he employed. A woman completely off limits.

And that was the category his mind had put her into: off-limits employee.

But if she were seeing someone, his plan wouldn't work.

Taking a deep breath, he decided to go for broke. "Are you seeing anyone?" he asked.

She had just taken a sip of water and now nearly choked.

"Me? Seeing someone?" She put the cap back on the bottle. "That's a personal question." She glanced around the room nervously as if expecting to be on camera and being punked. "There *might* be someone, but nothing concrete as of yet."

His jaw slipped open. So, there *had* been men, he'd just never noticed. He had never seen flowers on her desk, but then again, he'd never thought to look.

Deborah was always available. On hand for late-night meetings, early morning conference calls, last-minute business trips…always available for him and whatever he needed.

His head nodded like a jack–in–the–box as he thought how to proceed. She wasn't dating anyone right now. She was available.

"I gave much thought to our discussion earlier, and I think you're right."

Her eyebrow lifted. "I was, sir? Which discussion?"

His finger tapped his temple. "You have a good head for contemplating all the little details." He let out a slight chuckle, trying hard not to show how nervous he was. "I ran through every scenario in my head I could think of, and I have a proposition for you. I'm hoping you'll agree to the arrangement."

Deborah sat straighter and leaned in toward him, the leather of her chair seat squeaking. "Of course, sir. Whatever you need."

His finger danced around the paperwork on his desk in nervous little circles. "I need you to agree to be my wife."

She dropped the water bottle, and the plastic container made a thud when it hit the floor. Thankfully, the cap was still on. "You, you need me… you *want* to marry me?"

"No." His eyes widened, and he realized he had phrased the request poorly. "I need you to *pretend* to be my fiancée. Temporarily. Just so I won't be listed on the top ten bachelor list." He flipped over the paperwork and explained to her the terms of the agreement. She held each sheet of paper and carefully read the terms as he described them.

She appeared numb as he went over the details. He could tell she was trying hard to wrap her mind around the entire farce.

"So, I'm not being fired?" she said, her voice wavering.

"Hell, no," he quickly blurted out. He studied her face and eventually relief showed in her eyes. He couldn't function without her as his assistant. Why on earth would she assume he was letting her go?

"I'm giving you a paid vacation for doing me this favor." He pointed to the third page of the document. "You can even stay at the Langtham Hotel."

"The Langtham?"

Her jaw dropped and he wondered if she had ever stayed in such an elegant place before. Her expression told him that she was completely taken aback by his request.

"That's a nice hotel." The tone of her voice was low, and she sounded unsure of the proposal.

"Only the best. This lie needs to look real."

She fidgeted in her seat. "This seems so complicated. Telling the truth and getting out of this lie gracefully might be better."

He was already in too deep. He needed a miracle,

and that miracle was named Deborah. "The truth will make me look bad. Trust me, I can't think of any other way out of this situation."

"I hate lies." Her voice was deep and she enunciated each word, emphasizing the word hate.

He was sinking, with her taking away the life line.

"I hate lies, too. If you know of anything else I can do, now would be the time to tell me."

He watched as she wrung her hands and appeared deep in thought.

She eyed the paperwork. "For years I've been at your side. I don't think this is appropriate. I'm your assistant."

"You're the only one I can trust."

He never realized just how true that statement was before now. Crossing this line may put a strain on their work relationship, but he'd make it up to her. More time off. More pay. More...well, *fewer* personal errands. Less ignoring her. Less last-minute trips with her putting everything together for him.

He really needed to start treating her better. She was a staple in his life. He needed her and because of that, he needed to treat her *a lot* better.

He would make it all right. Somehow.

"You'll need me during those few weeks off. You have the new release coming out, all your appointments...the merger. How can I just take off?"

Remembering Scott's suggestion, Daniel asked, "Can't you hire me a temp employee?" He stood and came around the desk, taking a seat on the corner of it. "Other assistants take vacations that don't coincide with their boss's schedule. I'm sure temporary agencies are busy hiring out people to fill that role all the time."

She gave him what looked like a forced smile. "I'm sure that's true, but surely you could hire a temp employee to pretend to be your fiancée."

"I need someone I can trust." His voice sounding more needy than determined. He then pointed to the contract. "This document will keep a hired temp worker quiet, but…" He took a small box out of his suit's breast pocket and opened it, feeling his chest slightly tighten at seeing his grandmother's ring.

"The ring also has to look real. This was my grandmother's. I know I can trust you not to pawn it, or trade it, or lose it on purpose."

He held the box up for her to get a better view of the princess cut. Its facets caught in the overhead lighting and sparkled. Two carets exquisitely set in a beautiful setting. "The ring is insured, but it belonged to someone I cared about, and has sentimental value to me."

Her face paled into a what-have-I-gotten-myself-into expression.

The jewelry was not as fancy or extravagant as what he could afford now. His grandmother had given it to him in hopes that he'd one day ask a woman to marry him. Since he never planned to get married, this would be the closest thing to honoring the pledge.

Plus, his grandmother would have liked Deborah. Both women were strong, dedicated to family, and were trustworthy to a fault.

"It's beautiful," Deborah said, her voice cracking. With a shaky hand, she took the box.

She pulled her gaze away from the blink and looked up at him. "Your grandmother's?"

"On my mother's side."

She touched the box and studied the ring for a silent moment, which felt like torture for him.

"My life will need to be put on hold." She glanced at his desk calendar and then her eyes shifted, deep in thought. "I hadn't made any particular plans... although, I did agree to..."

"Agree to do what?" he asked.

"A date, of sorts." She bit her lower lip and looked more mentally between a rock and a hard place than he had ever seen her before.

He felt so close to closing the deal, he didn't need anything to go wrong. "You'll get some good time off."

"A vacation would be nice, those dates would be nice,..spending time with you would be..." She made eye contact, and a blush filled her cheeks. "I've never been to the opera before."

"You'll love it." He grabbed a pen and handed it to her, hoping that she was in the process of agreeing.

Her eyes narrowed with more unasked questions, which made the hairs stick up on the back of his neck. "There is to be no..." Her soft voice trailed off and she gestured between the two of them. "Nothing physical."

She was always a separation–of–business–and–pleasure type of person. She saw him as nothing more than her boss, and that was exactly what he needed right now. No feelings, no drama, no relationship.

Things needed to be perfectly clear. "Nothing physical between us." He pointed to the section of the contract address that. "Hand holding, chaste kissing, just a public show. I won't be joining you at the Langtham."

"Good." Her voice sounded decisive and he could see an invisible wall marking off new boundaries. "No hotel stay, no Alaskan honeymoon.... As long as we're clear. Nothing can ever happen between the two of us in any romantic way."

He stared at her fixed jaw and stiffened body. His reputation as a ladies' man was something worth bragging about, but Deborah didn't seem to care. In fact, it looked like the idea of dating him was actually distasteful to her.

The two of them were both roughly the same age, both physically well built, both educated. On paper, they made a good match. He glanced at her shapely body. Her figure was always hour-glass perfect, her clothing professional, and, even though he couldn't see them now under the table, he knew her legs were tanned and tone. Perhaps in the dating department, she thought she could do better than him?

An odd feeling took hold of him. It wasn't as though he wanted to be in the running for her affections, and yet, he didn't like the idea of not being invited to the race.

Then again, no one knew him as well as Ms. Baxter did. She knew about his rotating bedroom door and how women didn't stick around long enough for an anniversary.

Perhaps her lack of any romantic interest in him is what had made her such a great assistant all these years.

Her eyebrow rose, and he realized she was waiting for the next contractual commitment to drop.

"Deborah, please do me the honor of pretending to be my fiancée."

She pulled away, sitting farther back in her seat.

"I'll give you twice your Christmas bonus if you do it. I'll also make sure the scholarship is renewed each year, even if Josh doesn't take a full course load to meet the requirements."

Her eyes widened and she leaned forward. "I've always been able to trust you."

"Is that a yes?"

Her gaze drifted to the floor. "Shouldn't you be on one knee?"

His heart skipped a beat. Once again, Deborah

would get him out of a tight spot. This plan would work. He wouldn't be the target of a manhunt, he wouldn't be thrown into the dangerous waters of the general public, and he wouldn't be alone in any of this.

She would save him.

As he knelt on the floor and held up the ring, a strange feeling—powerful and strong—took hold of him. His mouth went dry, and a tightening in his chest surprised him. This was only a fake proposal. So why did it feel so real?

"Deborah, will you marry me?"

She held out her hand and allowed him to place the ring on her finger—a surprisingly perfect fit. "Of course, sir."

12

_____

"*I*n this section, Mr. Ellington agrees to pay you this dollar amount,"—Scott pointed to the figure on the page—"for fulfilling the duties of the contract."

Deborah was mistaken. Asking her to run interference with the press wasn't the weirdest thing Mr. Ellington had ever asked her to do. This contract and fake engagement were.

She took a deep breath and caught a glimpse of Daniel as he sat next to her. He was calm and collected. Is this how he was with every contract he signed? Dignified, focused, and having an 'eye of the tiger' effect? No wonder he did so well in business. He sat there looking like a statue, a very formidable one.

Scott tapped on the page with her pen and she focused back on the contract. The hefty sum on the paper stared up at her. It was a lot of money. Funds she needed for Josh. His scholarship would be secured, he wouldn't have to work two part-time jobs while attending school, and he wouldn't have to feel so guilty any time he asked her for money.

Naturally, she was happy to give him money for his books, for his food…she never once complained. Yet, somehow, Josh always felt bad about asking. He'd start off by asking for something like two-hundred dollars and within a couple of sentences be down to 'I can make due with just fifty, if you can spare it'.

There had also been talks of him taking a year off and working so he could pay cash for school without taking out loans. She didn't want to hear any of that. His future was at stake, and he needed an education.

She didn't want to be a mother that couldn't help her child out. This contract—this two-week contract —would solve so many of her problems.

Not agreeing to do this job seemed pointless, even silly.

Sitting across from Scott's desk had made the transaction feel so…real. And, fortunately, very formal. This was a legally-binding contract, not just a promise of payment for a favor. A promise could always be broken.

Money. Vacation. And, most importantly, securing Josh's education.

She could do this.

Scott pointed to the page. "Initial here."

She scrawled her *DB* where he had indicated and then took a sip of her water. The money amount was fine, the pleasantries, too. Scott highlighted one section of the document after another.

"Wardrobe allowance," he said, pointing to another amount on the page. "Miscellaneous spending money for tips and other such things. Mostly to flash in case the press discovers you're staying at the Langtham."

That was a lot of mad money, more than she would ever spend since it was so frivolous. Her foot shook under the desk, so she placed her hand on her knee to stop it. She needed to focus on the big picture. "Mr. Ellington said my son's scholarship…"

"It will be secured for him," Daniel said. "I believe it's on the next page."

"It is, but first…" Scott circled the last item on the current sheet of paper. "I need Ms. Baxter to sign here, saying that she won't sue the company or hold it, or you, responsible for any present or past emotional, mental, or financial anguish."

"Anguish?" Deborah eyed the page skeptically.

"Ms. Baxter, this is a fake proposal of marriage," Scott said, gaining her attention. "Mr. Ellington assured me that there is no romantic relationship between the two of you, and that there never has been. This engagement is only contractual. There is no promise of marriage here. No assurance of a relationship. No promise of love. And you can't keep his grandmother's ring."

Deborah felt the heaviness of the ring on her finger, and her cheeks blushed. She understood that this was all fake, but seeing Daniel on one knee, proposing…that was…well, nearly dream-perfect. But just a fantasy. Deborah could understand that some women could easily be swept away by such a sight, but not her. If Daniel ever had any romantic feelings for her, surely they would have surfaced over the last two decades of being in his employ.

"I understand that this is a fictitious relationship." She kept her voice light and pleasant, but didn't hold back the hint of sarcasm. "It's not like in the movies where I'll take off my glasses, and Mr. Ellington will swoon."

She let out a slight—yet nervous—giggle as she initialed the paragraph, barely glancing at the text.

Scott turned the page. "Your son, Joshua Baxter, will be allotted the full scholarship amount for the remaining three years he is in college. If he doesn't meet the minimum GPA criterion, Mr. Ellington will continue the scholarship payments from his own personal accounts. This amount will be paid to Joshua even if he chooses to transfer to another school, but he must remain in school to receive the money. The sum of which is $45,000. This will cover his remaining tuition. Mr. Ellington has also agreed to pay an additional $15,000 per year to your son for college living expenses."

Deborah stared at the total as she felt the air leave the room. Her son was getting a full ride to one of the best universities in Texas, and she didn't have to worry about him working while attending school. She didn't have to worry about going into debt to help him get his education. She didn't have to worry about anything.

Josh wouldn't drop out of school to work, either. This money would lock him in and ensure that he received his degree. It was the miracle she had prayed for.

She felt tears welling up but managed to hold them back and look at Daniel. "That is very generous of you."

The smile he gave her—sincere and sensitive—sent lightning bolts of emotion through her entire body. "You're the one doing me the favor," he said, his voice velvety and smooth.

His hand gently touched her shoulder. "I'm happy to take care of your son."

"This section covers the public displays of affection." Scott indicated a lengthy paragraph and his voice ran over the words. The description of what 'no sexual intercourse' meant actually made her blush, and it made her realize just how thorough a lawyer Scott was. He defined at least five different sexual acts before getting to the list of approved physical contact.

Not that she figured she and Mr. Ellington would engage in any such activity aside from hand holding.

"Discrete kissing is acceptable…," Scott continued.

Kissing. She took in a deep breath and glanced over to Daniel. His piercing blue eyes melted her, but what she now focused on were his soft, full lips. He would, at some point, kiss her. Not passionately. She understood that. But still, a kiss. Her foot, which had been behaving for the last few minutes, began its little dance under the table once again.

Daniel wore his dark gray suit with the power tie that always brought out the blue in his eyes. The whiskers of his five o'clock shadow covered his strong jaw and it gave him a rugged appearance.

A suit that said business, and a face that said playtime.

Yep. The whole package.

"Do you have any questions about the contract?" Scott asked.

Deborah sat straighter in the chair and took in a deep breath as she shook her head. She had just read the no-love clause, and was already having romantic thoughts? If there were anything between her and Daniel, it would have happened already. Daniel, though generous, had created this fake relationship thing for himself—for *his* gain. She was happy to help, but she needed to keep things in perspective.

"If you'll just sign at the bottom of the page, Ms. Baxter."

"Why do you need a picture of us?" Daniel asked once he had signed the document, as well.

Scott's gazed bounced from Daniel to Deborah and back again. "You said it yourself. Actually, I believe it was Deborah's suggestion. You'll need a picture to leak to the media."

Scott stored the documents in his desk and smiled back at them, giving the formal proceedings a more casual feel. "You got the ring. You got the girl. Now, we need to capture this happy moment for the world to see."

"I don't want anything leaked to the media." Daniel didn't need a personal picture of himself in the news. Even when it came time for company picture opportunities, he usually had the media display the company logo instead of his mug on the pages of their rags.

"We just need one image, something that we take and can control. A shot that clearly shows you and obscures most of Deborah's face but will satisfy the press so they won't hound you to pose for one."

"It's a good idea," Deborah said. "Just as long as you can't make out that it's me in the photo."

Scott stood up and looked around the room. "We'll only get part of your profile." He then pointed to the corner. "This place looks too much like an office, but the white wall will work."

He took his cell phone from his pocket, and Daniel cringed. How many times had people taken out there phones just to snap a picture of him? He had lost count.

"Daniel, stand over here and look at me. Deborah will face the wall."

This would be a close-up? Couldn't he just be a thumbnail, a tiny head on a blurred .jpg image? Daniel walked to the corner of the room, not sure how to pose. He wasn't even sure if Scott was a good photographer. Then again, if he weren't, a fuzzy image would suit him just fine.

"Take off your jacket," Scott said. "You look too business-like." When Daniel removed it, Scott added, "Take the tie off, as well. You look stuffy and formal."

"I *am* stuffy and formal."

Deborah held out her hand for his jacket. "You were the one who wanted this little charade, so behave and do what Scott suggests." Once he'd removed his tie, he handed them both to her.

Scott took them from her and placed them on the desk. "Deborah, your outfit is a bit too businessy, too.

Since you have a blouse under your blazer, let's lose your jacket, too."

Once off, Scott positioned her in front of Daniel, facing the wall. "I need you to turn your body just a bit, Deborah. I only want to see your side profile." He then studied the two of them. "Daniel, put your arm around her waist."

It was like Scott was positioning a doll. Deborah stood close enough for him to smell the faint scent of her perfume. She always wore a delicate scent and never allowed it to be overpowering in the office.

Taking a deep breath and puffing out his chest, he wrapped his hand around her slender waist, allowing her to take a step closer to him.

This was the nearest he had ever stood to her. The closest their bodies had ever been—except for maybe a few times when they'd stood in crowded elevators. During those times, he did his best not to think of her as a woman.

But, now, he enjoyed holding her close.

"Oh, the glasses. Remove them." Scott then pointed at her hair bun. "And let your hair down. It'll help to hide your face."

Deborah unpinned her hair and handed the clip and her specs to Scott. She then tousled her waves and gazed into Daniel's eyes. "This is that movie moment, Mr. Ellington." She mockingly shook her head like all the women did in the movies. "Do you feel any different?" The tone of her voice was

Marilyn Monroe breathy, but she soon started to laugh —her body moving slightly closer to his.

This was Ms. Baxter. His right-hand woman. His employee.

His Number One.

But she was a vision.

A vision with a sense of humor. Her lighter side was showing. He always enjoyed when she allowed herself to put her guard down. He found her playful sassiness very sexy.

Daniel's heart rate sped up, and a tightening occurred in his pants. A sensation that he had controlled around her for nearly two decades. One that he needed to control right now. She stood way too close, and he certainly didn't need her brushing up against him.

Her breath caressed his neck as she laughed. Her giggles were musical.

The only time she ever let her softer side slip was when they worked late into the early mornings. Those times, she'd be so tired and giddy, she was an entirely different person. She'd let herself enjoy the moment.

Daniel always had fun with this side of Deborah. It was the side he had always been attracted to, the one that he had always wanted to be closer to.

Her voice filled with more joy, and he stared at the twinkle in her eyes as the smile reached them. The curve of her cheeks, the fullness of her lips…her entire face was framed by her dark brunette hair in a way that he had never seen before.

She had a strong jaw, and high cheekbones—just like all the Hollywood starlets had back in the 1960s. He had noticed those fabulous features on Deborah years ago, but now, in her late thirties, they were striking.

Daniel let out a nervous chuckle just as Scott said, "Okay, I got it."

The two of them turned to see Scott, who was staring at his phone.

Deborah pulled away and began putting her hair back into its tight bun.

The moment was over, but it had been captured digitally for all time.

"This one is perfect." Scott turned the cell around and showed it to Daniel. "You look dead serious, but Deborah is…"

"Perfect," Daniel said. He then looked back at her. "Your face is covered. You can't really see who you are." He tapped Scott on the arm. "Good job."

Deborah replaced and buttoned her suit jacket. "I should call a temp agency and get a replacement secretary."

Scott waived her off. "That's already taken care of."

13

*D*eborah followed the GPS directions to the Langtham Hotel, relying on her car's guidance system to show her the way. The rental car was more luxurious than what she normally drove, but she was already playing her part.

The sun shone in from the side window of the car and reflected off the diamond ring weighing down her finger. Each time she shifted, she could hear its soft thump against the wheel, as well. His grandmother's wedding band...

She hadn't expected the ring's perfect fit.

The ring was beautiful, but to see Daniel down on one knee, proposing... Proposing, being engaged, getting married. She took a deep breath and reminded herself that it was all fake. Fake. Fake. Fake. Daniel had no romantic feelings for her, and he shouldn't. He was her boss. She was only doing what a good employee would do to help her boss.

There was no engagement, just a nice vacation and a beautiful hotel stay. That was it. Nothing more.

Focusing on the road, she saw the hotel in the distance. Diplomats and high executives stayed in such a fancy place, not single mothers who struggled to put a kid through college.

But for the next few days, she wasn't an assistant living paycheck–to–paycheck. She was to be a wealthy heiress, and she needed to play the part.

No book existed on how to live like the rich and famous, but she suspected they tipped well. When she'd deposited the check from Mr. Ellington, she dutifully withdrew cash for flashing. It wasn't as though she hadn't given well–deserved tips in the past, but it seemed silly to take out a few hundred dollars for tipping and mad money.

She pulled up to the grand building and, even though she never did this, she decided to valet her car. She had to get used to spending money, plus, Mr. Ellington would pay the bill.

She shook her head. Daniel. Daniel would pay the bill.

Damn. She had to get used to calling him by his first name.

An eerie sensation took hold of her, and she fought hard to shake it off. But she couldn't. Daniel could have asked *anyone* to be his fiancée. Hell, he could have hired anyone to play the part. But he had chosen *her*.

Maybe she shouldn't feel too... What was the word she was looking for? Proud? She wasn't sure, but she did feel excited. Energized in a giddy, schoolgirl way, and that was a feeling she hadn't had in a long time—if ever.

It was a feeling that she needed to keep in check, though.

We're just playing a role, she told herself. Nothing can—or should—happen between the two of them. Boss and employee was a bad combination.

But the idea of being Daniel's fiancée, even if just for pretend...she couldn't wipe the smile off her face. And the butterflies that fluttered in her stomach every time he called her by her first name? How could a man make a common name like *Deborah* sound so sexy?

She now thought about the rest of the charade. She was supposed to be a rich Austrian heiress.

Good Lord. When men fantasized, they went for large and stupid, didn't they? She couldn't just be a businesswoman? Or a famous author? A rich heiress certainly clued her in as to what Daniel really wanted. She had never known him to date anyone of royalty, but the man could certainly dream.

She pulled her car into the circular driveway toward a uniformed man, who immediately waved for a bellman and then walked to her car door and waited.

The moment was here. Two weeks of another life and all she needed to do was step out of the car and be transported into la–la land. She popped open the trunk, grabbed her purse, and opened the door. The doorman held out his hand to help her out.

"Welcome to the Langtham, ma'am."

She extended her ringed hand displaying her huge lie so he could help her out of the car. She then handed the keys into his expectant palm without engaging him in conversation, just dismissively smiling at him.

The bellman opened the trunk and pulled out her suitcases. She suspected she had packed too much but the spending allowance she had allowed her to buy an entirely new wardrobe. She could change into a new outfit several times a day and still not wear everything. Of course, she shopped for sales and didn't pay department store retail prices.

Opening the back door of the car, she picked up her computer bag. If she had to spend two weeks here, she could at least finish her latest novel. With the Ellington-Weston merger happening, she had very little time lately to write. Weekends and evenings were become scarce, and she really wanted to see where her characters were taking her story.

She took the valet ticket from the man and entered the hotel, her luggage following her. As she walked to the front desk, she heard her name being called.

Turning, she saw Caroline. Why was she here?

And, more to the point, why did she have such a huge grin on her face. Judging by the Starbucks cup in her hand, she had been here a while.

"Bridal Suite 2301." Caroline extended her hand and, Deborah assumed, slipped the bellman a tip. He said a quick, "Yes, ma'am," and then he left with the luggage.

"What are you doing here?" Deborah asked, thrilled to see a friendly face. A top–secret escapade never included a girl's coffee klatch, but she'd gladly take it.

Caroline looped one arm around Deborah's. "This is going to be so much fun!" She held up her cup. "Do you want to grab a coffee before going up to the room?"

Having someone to spend time with sounded nice, especially since she hadn't realized the vacation would include company, but a six-dollar cup of coffee was not something she ever did.

Until now.

Once Deborah got her coffee, and Caroline another decaf refill, Caroline tapped her watch. "We have an hour until our massages."

"Massages?" Deborah only wanted a little quiet time, perhaps to reflect on everything or maybe to write. She couldn't even remember the last time she'd had a massage.

"Naturally, we'll want to relax. There's no better way than to start with a nice spa day." The two walked to the elevator. "After the massage, we have appointments for our hair, nails, and makeup."

An expensive cup of coffee was one thing, but a spa day? Everything was happening too fast, and too expensively, for her taste. "None of this is necessary, Caroline."

Caroline gave her a wry smile. "You're getting an entire makeover. After all, you're soon to be Mrs. Daniel Ellington."

Deborah dipped her toes into the warm, soapy water and enjoyed the warmth of the swirling pedicure bath. She couldn't remember the last time she had had a spa day.

"Mmmmm," Caroline moaned. She sat next to Deborah in her own luxurious massage chair. "This is so worth it."

Spending hundreds of dollars to pamper herself was a luxury. One Deborah saw as a silly waste of money. Although, she *did* enjoy the moment.

"I'm glad you tagged along on my hotel stay." Deborah smiled at her friend.

"Oh, Deb. I wouldn't miss an opportunity like this."

The only thing Deborah had to do today was prepare for a fancy dinner tonight. The original plan was to lock herself away in the deluxe suite and crank out another couple of chapters. Thinking back to the grandness of the hotel and how delightful their spa services were, she'd have to make sure the heroine in her novel visited a place like this.

Actually, Deborah could use future spa days as a tax deduction and site that she was doing research. She let out a chuckle. If that were the case, her next book would be in the setting of Hawaii.

Glancing at her gel–painted nails, and admiring how beautiful they looked, she heard Caroline calling her name.

"We got the deluxe package, including waxing."

Waxing? That sounded painful, and it was something Deborah had never done before. "I'm fine without it."

The pedicurist tapped Deborah's right leg, signaling that she needed it out of the water. The woman then pointed to her forehead and asked, "We can do your eyebrows too."

"We'll take everything," Caroline said to the woman.

Deborah recognized and didn't care for the upsell. "The eyebrows stay." She glanced down at her only half–shaven legs. The wintry season called for pants or long skirts. She had shaved only up to her knee, and that was two days ago. The pedicurist, who now massaged Deborah's leg, had a prickly mess to deal with. They definitely needed attention.

But it wasn't as though Daniel—she caught

herself mid-thought. It wasn't as though *any* man was going to notice, let alone touch, her legs.

She took a deep breath and gazed at the ceiling. She couldn't allow her mind to slip, not like that, not after all of these years. It was her dark secret; one she wouldn't repeat.

"I have to say, I was surprised to hear that you'd agreed to this deal," Caroline said.

"Daniel needed my help, that's all." Deborah glanced down at the woman seated at her feet, knowing full well that they listened to every word their clients said. Perhaps it was time for a change of topic.

"I am sorry, though," Deborah said.

"For what?"

"I told you I was ready for the blind date you wanted to set me up with. Now, that will have to wait until after…after everything is done with the contract."

Caroline waved her manicured hand. "Don't worry about it. The guy I have in mind is perfect for you so I have a feeling things will work out." Her voice sounded so self-assured, and the expression on her face told Deborah that Caroline truly believed she had found 'the one' for her.

Highly doubtful.

The jets hit Deborah's toes and felt like angels massaging her toes. "Who do you have in mind?" she asked in between coos of contentment.

Caroline's lips curled up into a wicked smile. "You'll have to wait and find out. He's busy at the moment, so waiting two weeks won't be an issue." She now studied Deborah. "How long have you worked at *the company*?"

Glancing down at the pedicurists, Deborah noted the two were focused on their job and not interested in chatting with them. Which was good.

"Nearly twenty years."

"Wow," Caroline said. "Did you start working there after high school?"

Deborah lay back heavier in her chair and allowed the massage rollers to better hit the base of her neck. "I knew there was a reason I liked you."

"Seriously. Is this the only job you've ever had?"

She shrugged. "The only job I ever needed. The pay is good, although the hours can sometimes be rough." Overall, they weren't too bad but there had been several late-night hours and early morning breakfast meetings, as well as some weekend crunch-mode sessions to get work done. Other than trying to juggle the schedule with getting her sister Sue to babysit Josh, the extra hours never really bothered her.

"I can understand rough hours. Being a waitress was no picnic before I met Scott."

It was one reason Deborah felt close to her friend. The woman hadn't been a spoiled rich kid with a trust fund. She'd worked hard to make ends meet, and had put herself through school. Caroline had been a true rags-to-riches story with a Prince Charming.

Caroline pulled her foot from her pedicurist's hands. "No, you can't massage my feet. Please just pumice and paint." The woman wiped the lotion off her hands and then grabbed a clean towel to dry Caroline's foot.

"It's a shame pregnant women can't have their feet and ankles massaged." Deborah let out a soft moan as her woman now rubbed hers. "This feels amazing."

"Don't rub it in." Caroline hugged her large belly. "It's worth it."

"That's right." Deborah smiled, remembering her time being pregnant with Josh. She vomited pretty much every day, but once you hold the baby in your arms nothing else but that blessing matters. "Your entire world will be that baby. Motherhood was the best thing I ever did."

"I hope you don't mind me asking," Caroline said, "but, whatever happened to Josh's father?"

Thinking about him, and trying to remember the man's good qualities, Deborah decided not to mentally chastise herself for making such a poor choice all those years ago. He may have been handsome and successful, but that was it. What was on the inside is what mattered most, and that man was hollow.

"He died years ago," she lied. Although, to her, he *was* dead.

"I'm so sorry. He must have been young. Was it a car accident?"

If it were possible to die from being an asshole, he would have died long ago. "Natural causes. He was older than I was. We were never together since he wasn't a family man."

"You never married him?" Her voice wasn't accusative or sharp, but filled with empathy in a supportive way used by best friends. Her concern brought a warm fuzzy feeling to Deborah that she normally didn't have when someone asked her about Josh's father.

Caroline added, "I assumed you were divorced."

"It's always just been Josh and me." And now, with Josh away at college, Deborah's world had narrowed in on her. It was frightening, but she was adjusting one day at a time.

"But you've dated. Had relationships."

Deborah watched as the pedicurist now dried her feet. She asked about the nail polish color, which was a bright, fire engine red.

"Right?" Caroline asked again when she got no answer.

Deborah nodded. "I've dated a few men. They were never quite right," she said, not wanting to go into any lengthy detail. After Josh was born, she had a newborn to care for. She figured she'd be able to date once he went off to kindergarten, but that didn't happen. Once Josh started asking about his father she figured she'd start dating again, but those conversations were just awkward with her telling him mostly the truth, but keeping her secret to herself.

Even after he had graduated from high school and had moved away, she was an empty-nester and free to go out whenever she wanted. She just hadn't met anyone of interest to go out with.

"I guess it is harder to find a man when you have a child to raise." Caroline now admired her freshly painted toes. "Who would be your Mr. Right if you could build him from scratch?"

Deborah smiled at the thought. Making your man from top to bottom sounded nice. "I guess someone I can talk to. Someone who is charming and can get me to laugh." She bit her lip and focused on what she really wanted. "Someone who respects me and can support me."

She shook her head. "I mean. I don't mind working. In fact, I enjoy it. But I'd like the opportunity to do more writing and see if there is a future in it for me."

"That's right. You're a writer," Caroline said. "I searched for your book, but I didn't find it."

Naturally, she wouldn't. That's why pen names existed. How could she write about a series of billionaires who fall in love with their assistants and not make it seem autobiographical? No one she knew would ever read her novels. "Don't worry about it."

She motioned with her hand in a karate–chop way. "I try to keep my life divided and separate."

"That's probably a smart idea," Caroline said.

Deborah needed to change the subject. "Do you read much?"

"Some," Caroline said. "What about physical looks? What would your ideal date look like?"

At the very least the topic was back on perfect dates and not her books. Deborah would just die inside if anyone she knew read her novels.

She rarely opened up and talked about such things as the perfect man, but then again, she didn't have many girlfriends to hang out with. And, with the smell of nail polish hanging in the air, it didn't get much more stereotypical Girls' Day Out than this—unless they went upstairs and had a pillow fight.

"Well?" Caroline's gazed studied Deborah. "I think I have the perfect blind date for you, I just need to know physically what you're interested in."

Deborah's gave a half-way shrug. "I guess my ideal man would be tall and have dark hair. I'd want him to be smart and sophisticated. Someone who helps others, or contributes to charity." A smile crossed her lips as she stared blankly off into the distance. "I love piercing blue eyes and a strong jaw. Ripped muscles… I wouldn't say no to those either."

Letting out a slight chuckle, Deborah shook her head. "I can hear it, so you don't need to tell me. I just described Superman."

"No, you just described Daniel."

Her gaze darted to the floor, and she found it difficult to make eye contact with Caroline. A fake smile plastered onto her face. "No. That's not who I'm describing." She took a deep breath and sensed the awkward silence in the room.

"I guess," Deborah said, her mind racing to backtrack. "I mean… As a personal assistant, you spend time with a man. You take care of his home, get his clothing laundered, buy him new socks when the old ones get frayed… You even do his banking because he trusts you. It doesn't mean there is anything… There *isn't* anything…"

"You did accept this contract, Deb."

Caroline stared at Deborah as if waiting for a confession. There was none to give, except the truth. In a dismissive tone Deborah said, "I agreed because I can use the money. College doesn't pay for itself. Daniel's offer was very generous."

Caroline sat straighter in the chair. Her foot moved and messed up the work of the pedicurist, causing the woman to curse under her breath. "Speaking of Daniel, I almost forgot." She carefully picked up her phone. "We're still getting our hair done today and—"

Deborah touched her hair, which was classically pulled back into a professional bun. "You want me to cut my hair?"

"Cut and dye." Caroline's head tilted as she stared

at Deborah's hair. "You're practically my age, and you have gray."

She felt the blush on her face. "I have a good ten years on you."

"You couldn't tell. You're a stunning woman, Deb. You should pamper yourself sometimes."

The compliment was doubly nice coming from Caroline, who had porcelain beautiful skin and gorgeous blonde hair. "I grayed early. Plus, dark brunette hair shows the gray more."

"We'll also give you a modern hairstyle."

"I don't know if I need to cut—"

"Deborah." Caroline voice was motherly-stern. "Your hair is comfortable, but it isn't attractive. You have so much to offer. You're brilliant, kind… available. Don't you want to make a good first impression when I set you up on the blind date later?"

Deborah hadn't thought of all the effort needed to get back into the dating game. But it was time for a new look. And what better time for a change than with her best friend. "I guess you're right. No point in wasting a perfectly good spa day."

"That's the spirit. You'll have a lovely evening out and enjoy yourself." She carefully typed on her phone. "I need to leak your picture and dinner reservations to the press tonight. That way, you can make an appearance."

"An appearance? Honestly, it's only a meal." A

nice quiet meal with Daniel sounded nice, but a media frenzy sounded horrific.

"Have you ever dined at Mas Rafs?" When Deborah shook her head, Caroline added, "It's an experience. I had to guess your size, but there are three gowns in the closet upstairs for you to choose from."

"Gowns?" This dinner seems more complicated than it needed to be.

Caroline glanced at her rounded belly. "They're not going to fit me again for a while. You might as well get some use out of them." She then grinned from ear–to–ear. "Just wait. It's going to be an evening you'll never forget."

———

14

*D*aniel's office door slammed open, jarring him from his concentration on the upcoming conference in Los Angeles.

Brian Compton stood in the doorway, his ego blocking most of the threshold.

Finally. Daniel had been waiting for a visit from Mr. Compton for days. He closed the file he was reading and put his computer in sleep mode to prevent any information from being seen. He trusted Mr. Compton, but only to a certain point.

"You can't just barge in..." a shrilly voice sounded from the other room. A second later, the temp secretary, Ms. Ortiz, stood with her hands on her hips, glaring at the man.

"He just barged in here." Her expression of a second grader tattling on a classmate fit her personality and grated against Daniel's nerves.

She stood her ground and puffed up her chest, allowing her see–through top to gape and show even more cleavage.

"Daniel..."

"Mr. Ellington," Daniel said, correcting her once more with a sterner tone. The girl was maybe twenty, and he suspected had never worked before. When he had asked for a mature, competent woman, the agency must have heard young and horny.

"Mr. Ellington, this man"—her eyes narrowed and shifted toward the intruder—"demands to talk to you and says it's a private matter."

Mr. Compton's eyebrow rose and he gave Daniel an all-knowing look, like he knew Daniel would drop everything and talk to him.

Bold and obnoxious. Those were the words Daniel would use to describe his personal private eye. Over the years, hiring the man had come in handy. Not even Ms. Baxter knew what he did.

"He doesn't have an appointment." The assistant's voice was laced with an undertone of a whine.

"See that we're not disturbed." Daniel crossed the room and gave the man a hearty handshake. He then closed the door, even while his secretary muttered something under her breath.

"Have a seat." Daniel gestured to the guest chair in front of his desk as he walked and returned to his own.

Brian pulled a large brown envelope from his

satchel. "The new gal is quite young, but a looker," he said, nodding his head back to the outer office.

In an all–business voice, Daniel said, "You have information for me." Daniel found it best not to be chatty with someone whose services cost three hundred dollars an hour.

Brian tossed the envelope on the desk. "Brandelynn Myers is a crafty one."

Daniel opened the envelope and took out the report. Her initial inspection months ago had pulled up nothing, but the expression on Brian's face told Daniel that, this time, something *had* turned up. "You discovered more since your first search seven months ago?"

Brian pointed to the paperwork and sneered. "Brandelynn Myers is her real name, but she has several aliases. A new one, Brandi Orson, works at the Black Cat Gentlemen's Club. She's been working there for quite some time."

He had been played.

Acid rose in his throat and he needed an antacid.

Deep down he had always known something wasn't quite right about Brandelynn. The feeling had lurked in his mind but he had been too blindsided by her body to take heed.

He scanned the document, first looking at the pictures. The eight–by–ten glossy images of her half naked and twirling on a pole and doing lap dances were enough to sicken him. Even with the jet–black wig she wore, he easily recognized Brandelynn. That body. Those curves. It was definitely her. "Working at a nightclub under an alias isn't a crime."

"No, but swindling wealthy men out of their fortunes is."

Daniel's jaw clenched and his anger grew, but this was why he paid so much for Brian's services.

"What do you mean?"

Brian leaned back in his chair, arms crossed. "She and her brother, Phillip Myers, are con artists. They settle in, find the richest man around, and take them for all they've got. That file has police records and warrants in Nebraska for her arrest. Their last scam almost landed her in jail."

"What about him?" Daniel held up a picture of Phillip. The image just had a hint of a side profile, not much to really go on.

"Phillip is squeaky clean. A pillar in journalistic circles. He gets her to do the dirty work."

Enough documentation lay in the dossier that the information should have been discovered months ago. "Why didn't any of this show up during your initial review of Brandelynn?"

"I almost didn't find it now. She's been clever with her aliases and always works for cash. Your tip of the Black Cat club is what clued me in."

Daniel shifted through the paperwork, grateful that he'd caught another social piranha. They were all money-hungry animals, ready to prey upon him.

Brandelynn and her brother hadn't been the first ones to try to scam him, but they had gotten farther with their plot than anyone else.

"When I initially ran the report for you," Brian said, "Brandelynn lived at the Century Heights condos."

Daniel recognized the place. He had picked her up there for their dinner the other night and several times before, as well—while she stood outside the building. "Let me guess. She doesn't live there."

"She rented a condo for only two months. My guess is that she suspected you'd run a search on her, and she covered her tracks to look as good as she could. She actually lives with her brother just outside the city in a trailer park."

"Of course they do." Daniel stared at one of the pictures. Brandelynn's beady eyes stared back at him and he could feel the bile building within his stomach.

Brian leaned in. "One of Phillip's aliases has allowed him to have a career as a tabloid editor. He makes decent money traveling around the country working on electronic publications, with Brandelynn following and conning rich men. My guess is that the two of them want more than just decent wages."

No official one-percenters club existed, but Daniel knew he couldn't let the pair attack another wealthy man. People like Brandelynn and Phillip are why the rich hire body guards and private detectives. "How do we make them both pay? I've never seen her brother."

He pointed at the image of the man in front of him. "This picture is too grainy and doesn't show enough to truly identify the man."

"I'm glad you mentioned that." Brian took out his phone. "This was found on Brandelynn's computer." He pressed a button and turned the screen so Daniel could watch.

Daniel's image was centered on the screen. "That's Mas Raf's restaurant. We went there for Valentine's Day." He glanced up at Daniel. "They recorded the dinner? Where was the camera hidden?"

"The floral center piece. Just keep watching."

Daniel watched the video in fast motion as Brian sped up the playback. The salad and then the dinner courses were served. Again, he watched as both couples got engaged. His face in the video cringed, which surprised him since he thought he had hidden his emotions well that night.

And then the fight began. Daniel didn't need to relive that moment. "I know we fought…"

"Here, this is what I want to show you." Brian changed the recording to play at normal speed.

Brandelynn sat alone, her gaze following Daniel as he left the private dining room. The expression on her face was disappointment fueled by what Daniel could only call rage. He initially didn't see her reaction because that night when he left, he didn't even glance back.

She was joined at the table by their waiter.

David paused the video. "He's in disguise, but that's her brother Phillip."

Daniel's head tilted as he leaned in and studied the man's face. He never would have suspected the man to be in costume, but then, he wasn't really paying attention to the wait staff that night.

"What the hell happened?" Phillip said on the recording.

"Game over."

He sat down. "You mean with all that," he said in a harsh tone, gesturing at her young, size–two body and D–cup boobs, "and with the other couples proposing, you couldn't force him to pop the question?"

Brandelynn looked defiant. "He told me he didn't see us ever getting married, and then he broke up with me."

Phillip's eyes narrowed and his hands balled into fists. "He was on the line, you were reeling him in, and then you let him get away!"

"This isn't my fault! He was way too young for this scam."

After a slight pause, Phillip eventually nodded. "We just wasted seven fucking months and the potential of a huge pay day with this damn list."

Brandelynn's eyes shifted downward and she didn't look at her brother.

"Good Lord." Phillip glanced around the

restaurant and then lowered his voice. *"Don't tell me you have feelings for the old coot."*

"Of course not!"

"You better not. We need to regroup. See if we can snag him back on the line."

Brandelynn shook her head and half-way rolled her eyes. *"He claims to have another woman."*

"Impossible."

"He says he's engaged."

Phillip glared at her. *"Go home. We'll talk tomorrow."* Phillip began to stand, but Brandelynn pulled him back down.

An evil grin then crossed her face. *"We may still be able to play Daniel, at least for a smaller stake."* When her brother's face lit up, she added, *"But promise me you'll make a big announcement in your online magazine. I'm talking really big."*

"What have you got in mind?"

"We're either going to catch Mr. Daniel Ellington in a lie or make his life and his new bride's very miserable."

Compton stopped the recording. "That's as good of a confection as you'll ever hear."

It was good, and that conversation explained so much to Daniel. "She's a good actress. I nearly believed she had feelings for me."

Compton pocketed his phone. "I believe she does. Her expression and the way she didn't make eye contact with her brother…she cares for you."

Daniel didn't want to believe it. She was cold and calculating, nothing more.

"I left her place as is. She'll never know I was there." He tapped his pocket where he had placed his phone. "Or that we have this confession."

A smile spread across Daniel's face. He hated being played, but now he had the upper hand. "Thanks, Brian."

"I suggest you contact the authorities and," he pointed out the closed door, "have your security on the lookout for her. If she does have feelings for you, she may approach you again. You need to be prepared to deal with her."

It'd be nice to get them both behind bars, but Brandelynn needed to pay. He'd make sure of that. Nobody made a fool of him and got away with it.

"The other item you requested is in there, as well. I'm assuming it's for research."

"Thanks for the work." Daniel removed a small white envelope from his desk drawer and handed it to the man. "It's all there, and then some."

The man accepted the payment and let himself out of the room, closing the door behind him.

Daniel sat, deep in thought. He knew he'd have to review the report from front to back to find out exactly how he could use the information. He had a friend down at police headquarters. If Brandelynn did come back, perhaps the officials could follow her and capture both her and her brother.

He reached into the envelope and pulled out the extra item. It was last month's issue of *Self–Made Diva* magazine.

He smiled as he read the headline, *"Is your boss a tyrant?"*

Daniel tossed the magazine into his desk drawer, and slammed it shut.

He was ***not*** a tyrant.

Asking an assistant for a cup of coffee didn't mean he belittled Ms. Baxter in any way.

And no personal errands? She was a *personal* assistant. Of course, she would run personal errands for him.

He had no time to thoroughly read an article that accused him of being an office Neanderthal. He also didn't want to pay someone to deliver the rag to him each month, especially at Brian Compton's rate of pay.

The fine print at the bottom of the page showed him the solution. There was an app?

He grabbed his phone and downloaded it. The magazine logo soon appeared, and the ezine had the same types of articles as the paper version. But there was a little more.

He grabbed his glasses and read the name of a tab on the site. *"What's trending."* He pressed the tab, and a window popped up asking him for push notifications.

And now, thanks to Scott, he knew what 'push notifications' meant.

Stupid technology. These gadgets changed every year. He hated how quickly everything changed, but the fluidity of the security market kept him in business. Every new app, every new gizmo, every new operating system created new potential security risks. Building an empire protecting people was the name of the game, and he played to win.

Getting the top news articles on his phone seemed like a time saver. Now he wouldn't have to waste time digging for the information in the paper magazine. Plus, he wouldn't be embarrassed by buying the stupid thing.

He squinted, looking at the information on this phone. Even swishing the screen larger, the text was tiny. He'd have to install it on his tablet.

He picked up his tablet, only to find it inoperable thanks to some coffee that had spilled on it this morning.

Goddamit.

He had loaded the merger paperwork on it and needed to review the details. The tablet was frozen and none of the buttons he pushed helped, not even the reset one.

He needed help, and the only person he could think of sat just outside his office—the one who'd spilled the coffee in the first place. He pressed a button on his desk phone and called her, only halfway grateful when she appeared in his doorway to offer help.

If the report hadn't been uploaded to the broken tablet, he would have just ordered a new iPad from supply. "Do you know anything about fixing broken tablets?"

Ms. Ortiz walked behind Daniel's desk and picked up the device. She then took it over to the window, leaned against the broad sill, and allowed her skirt to ride up—giving him a good view of her upper thighs.

The sun silhouetted her through the sheer blouse she wore, and he suspected the outfit selection was not by accident.

He didn't, and would never, date a woman from work—not that he was tempted by Ms. Ortiz; just upset that she thought her obvious ploys would work.

Did she think he'd throw her onto his desk, pull up her skirt, and pound into her?

Lawsuits galore. No, thank you.

The rumors of his uncle, Carl Weston, were legendary. The company had nearly shut down its doors due to lawsuits early on because of the man's lewd behavior. The man chased, and caught, many secretaries in his day.

Ms. Ortiz now held up the tablet did an Etch–A–Sketch shake to it. The silly maneuver almost had him laugh out loud.

"You have a digitizer problem, causing the LCD to fail." She blew air on the top of the display.

Maybe he was just cursed.

She fanned herself with the tablet as if the room suddenly became warmer. "The display keeps trying to turn on." One hand unbuttoned the top button on her blouse as she complained about the temperature of the room.

He didn't find the office all that warm, and, wasn't this the start of a porno movie?

"This model freezes sometimes. You just need to hit these two buttons together." She messed with the machine. "There!" She smiled as she walked back to him, placed her hand on his shoulder, and gave him the now rebooting device.

He let out the breath he didn't know he'd been holding. He needed this document for his next meeting, and he was impressed that Goldilocks had managed to get anything done.

She moved closer to him. "It'll come up soon," she whispered into his ear.

"Ms. Ortiz…"

"Call me Suzy, Daniel."

His skin crawled.

"My name is Mr. Ellington." His face hardened and he walked back to his chair and sat. "Ms. Ortiz, I have a meeting with Mr. Solomon and Mr. D'Eith this afternoon."

"Is that how you say their names?" she asked

through fits of laughter, her hand covering her mouth. "I called them solo–man and death when they got here."

Daniel's gaze darted to her. "They're here?"

"They arrived a while ago. They're sitting in my office."

He looked at his watch. The two men were early, and the temp had not only kept them waiting, she probably hadn't offered them a beverage either. Not that her coffee was anything to brag about.

He crossed the room to the wooden valet to get his jacket. "Please, let them in."

"Okay. Is there anything else you want me to do while you're in the meeting?"

His schedule was a mess, his office in disarray, and he had already caught her flirting with the CTO of the company during their morning appointment. It seemed that any rich man caught her attention.

Her fingers twirled a lock of her hair. "Just name it. I can do many things."

The thought of handing her the temporary agency's business card and asking for her to call in a replacement crossed his mind. But she'd probably mess that up, too. Besides, he wanted the satisfaction of letting the woman go. "Just let the gentlemen in, and close the door behind you on your way out."

.

---

15

*T*he work day was finally behind him, and Daniel just wanted to leave the office, go home, and relax. But since the temp had already left, he had to stay and check his schedule. Find out what his morning would be like, who he was meeting with, and what needed to be done. Goldilocks had left early and said she'd be in a little late tomorrow morning. Without her personal contact information, he would have no way of contacting her if needed.

Was this the work ethic these days? Or, was she just the worst of the lot? Deborah's son had interned here for the last couple of years, and he'd never behaved like this temp secretary.

Just as he was about to open his calendar app, his phone chirped and he read the notice. *'Dinner with Ms. Baxter'*. Dining reservations were something that Deborah would have mentioned to him as he prepared to leave for the day. She'd then stay and tidy up the place.

At least she had placed their fake dates on his calendar for reminders before leaving for the hotel.

Deborah always thought of everything, and always went that extra mile. She made his life easier.

God, he missed her.

He missed how she handled the office, handled the big brass, and handled…him. She always knew what to say and do to make the workplace more enjoyable.

The office lights were still on, and he assumed the phone service was not switched to nighttime mode. With director heads all across the world—since this was a global economy—those phones needed to be on so he could be contacted in case of an emergency.

How did he even turn them on?

Dirty glasses and coffee cups still rested on the bar. How long did Deborah usually stay in the evenings?

Paperwork spilled from his messy desk. Most likely, that was one more thing she took care of.

He grabbed the documents and neatly stacked them, making sure to lock anything in his desk drawer that was marked "Confidential."

The pretend engagement contract still lay on his desk. He couldn't file it with any of his company's paperwork, so he placed it in the wall safe where it would be secure. Scott had anticipated everything with that document, and his wife, Caroline, seemed eager to help out.

Such great friends.

Daniel's brow furrowed. Hadn't Scott said his baby was due in a few weeks? He was unsure if Deborah had already bought a gift for the baby… but that seemed so impersonal. On his way home tonight, he'd have to stop off at a baby store and get the couple something nice. Something hand–selected and bought by him felt more personal than having his assistant pick it out, or just clicking a few buttons and ordering something over the Internet.

Deborah had other things on her mind right now. She didn't need to be running his personal errands right now.

He asked his phone for the information to a nearby baby store. He had a rental car; he could handle this.

Loneliness overtook him as he walked past her empty desk. Paperwork lay all over it, including the inner-office mail and documents marked confidential.

The reminder on his phone buzzed again.

Shit.

He stuffed all the important documents into a desk drawer. There had better be nothing critical for him to look at tonight.

Deborah sat at the hotel bar feeling stupid, silly, and sexy. A dressed-up doll that remained on a shelf that no one touched.

The borrowed gown fit too tightly across the chest, which showed a bit too much cleavage, but overall, gave her a princess going to a ball feeling.

Her fingers glided over the beaded silk, admiring the delicately detailed work. It was wedding dress quality, except for it being a beautiful shade of green, not white. She suspected the matching necklace and earrings held real emeralds.

She touched the dangling gemstones to make sure they were still there. The chain lay heavily around her neck, but the earrings she wore felt light. Since the set had probably cost as much as one of her paychecks, she repeatedly checked that they still hung from her ears.

She felt uneasy with all the makeup she wore, and her new hairstyle felt too short. She nearly hadn't recognized herself in the mirror.

The stole, which she assumed was mink, lay across her shoulders. Some women loved the look and feel of fur, but it had never been of interest to her. She loved animals too much to wear them. Caroline had sworn that it was a good fake and hadn't brought any other jacket to match the gown, and Deborah needed *something* warm to wear—even if she questioned its man-made and synthetic quality.

Heaven knew her gown's bodice would leave her

chest exposed to the outside elements. She needed something warmer to wear. Sexy dresses were one thing, but common sense and a good quality coat were more appropriate.

Deborah took money from her green, beaded purse—enough for the Sprite and a generous tip—and placed it on the table. She then sipped her drink and kept an eye on the hotel's lobby. Mr. Ellington... Daniel...

Dammit.

She needed to be more careful and call him by his first name.

Daniel should be here soon.

She never called him by his first name—at least not out loud. It did suit the man, but calling him Daniel sounded more casual...more intimate...than she was used to. At least for the next few weeks, she'd need to get accustomed to calling him that.

She shifted in her seat and crossed her legs, feeling the smoothness of the waxing job. What a painful experience.

Her foot shook under the table, and she mentally told herself to calm down. She saw Daniel every day so tonight would be no different. She brushed her fingers through her new hairstyle, missing her usual twisted bun.

The bartender, dressed in black slacks, a green polo, and a white apron, approached her table. "This is from the gentleman at the end of the bar." He placed a coaster and napkin on the table and then put an amber colored cocktail atop it. The smell of alcohol wafted from the tiny glass.

At first, she figured the offering was a mistake. After all, men didn't buy her drinks. But when she glanced at the man, he held up his own glass as if toasting her.

She immediately looked away and stared at the beverage. Should she accept the drink? Naturally, she wouldn't drink it. Perhaps sending it back with the bartender would be more proper.

But the bartender had already left, making the decision for her, so Deborah smiled at the man and mouthed the words, "Thank you."

Shit.

He was heading her way.

A heaviness settled within her chest and she felt like a trapped animal.

She glanced at the lobby, but Daniel wasn't there yet. She gently touched the necklace once again. She'd be okay. It wasn't as if this man were coming to rob her, not with so many witnesses.

No, he was coming to share a drink with her. She took a deep breath, thinking it'd be better if he just stole the jewelry and ran.

"May I join you?" The man smiled and gestured to the chair across from her.

Butterflies fluttered in her stomach. She wasn't attracted to the man and didn't want his company, but it had been years since a man had approached her like this. "I'm waiting for someone," she said with the best smile she could muster on her face.

He sat down anyway. "I'll keep you company until they arrive."

She straightened in her chair and glared at him. "My date will be here shortly," Deborah said, hating the man's rudeness.

She studied the man's face. He couldn't be older than late twenties. Did he have any idea she was pushing forty? If he did, she suspected he wouldn't be sitting at this table. Or, could he be on the prowl for a cougar?

"Your eyes are beautiful."

As if the man could even tell what color they were since he stared at her cleavage. Or, was he staring at the necklace? Maybe he had pegged her for a wealthy woman who would be easy to take advantage of.

She now understood how Daniel felt when he was out and approached by strangers. Fur coat. Expensive jewelry. Designer gown. She was nothing more than a price tag.

"You're the most gorgeous woman I've every laid eyes on." His smile broadened. There was something about the gleam in his eye that told her that he genuinely found her attractive.

Perhaps she just needed to accept the compliment and stop letting her imagination run wild.

He gestured to the drink he'd bought her, the

coldness of it beading condensation and dripping down the glass to the coaster below. "Let's toast to your beauty and to our chance meeting."

"I'm sorry, but I don't drink." She gazed at the vastness of the marble–floored lobby entrance once again, hoping to see Daniel.

No such luck.

16

$\mathcal{D}$aniel was running late and driving slightly faster than usual. A prickling sensation tugged at the back of his neck. He was being followed.

Shifting lanes, he checked for any copy-cat cars, but saw none.

He took a deep breath to shake off his nerves. No one knew his schedule for tonight, other than when he would arrive at the restaurant, so he should be fine.

He suffered from stress. Nothing more.

Plus, the short stop at the baby store had taken much longer than he expected. Who would have guessed the Everything Baby store would be a madhouse?

After fighting traffic and nearly running a red light, he parked his Lexus in a short–term parking spot outside the hotel. He saw no one around and was thrilled that if the press was following him, that they hadn't discovered that he was headed to the Langtham to pick up his date. He wanted the mob at the restaurant, but not here. Giving Ms. Baxter... Deborah privacy was important to the success of the lie.

No one needed to know she was staying at the Langtham. After all, he wouldn't be staying the night. The press didn't need to know every detail of his fake engagement.

He entered the hotel and made his way to the bar. Several people sat on stools and side tables, but he didn't see Deborah anywhere.

Deborah would most likely be alone reading a book or something while she waited. She'd probably stick out like a sore thumb, and yet, he didn't see her anywhere.

He checked his watch. He'd arrived a couple of minutes late. What seemed odd was that she was always on time, if not early. He scanned the room again.

From the corner of his eye, a vision of beauty caught his attention. A brunette sat with a man near the front of the bar. Daniel couldn't see her face, but that hair... the dark ringlets reminded him of his dream woman from the other night.

That exceptionally erotic dream, the one he kept thinking about.

His eyes wandered from her shoulder–length,

soft–looking hair to her shoulders and ample chest. She nearly popped out of the dress she wore, and he got an eyeful of her creamy, alabaster skin. Her legs were crossed, and from where he stood, the angle of his vision could see a portion of her upper thigh through the dress's slit. Her shapely figure was curved in all the right places.

The woman brushed her hand through her dark, brunette hair, and he got a good look at her face. Her pert little nose, her shining green eyes, her flawless skin…she was a vision.

Even without his glasses on, he could tell she was a mature woman, not one of the many young women he had preferred so far. Her appearance was that of a thirty–something–year–old.

Could that be the problem? Was his dream woman more mature and sophisticated than what his little head generally desired? Was that what had made his dream so exciting? He couldn't remember the last time he had dated someone who was over thirty.

He moved closer to the table, feeling drawn to her. She sat tall in her chair, not making eye contact with her date. Her 'don't mess with me' body language gave off a sexy vibe, probably the opposite of what she intended since Daniel overheard her repeatedly ask the man across from her to leave.

Wait.

Daniel's head craned around to get a better look at

the woman's face now that he stood closer. Her voice sounded so familiar that he was sure he knew her.

He now stood close enough to stare at the woman. It was Deborah.

Her flawless skin. Her dark hair. Her lyrical voice.

She was stunning.

His gaze took in the sight of her whole body. Poised and perfect. Delicate and delightful.

She was a vision, but her companion was clearly annoying her.

Rarely did Daniel ever see Deborah flustered and uncomfortable, but the expression on her face showed her uneasiness. She wanted the man to leave, and the guy deliberately continued to hit on her and ignore her requests.

With each step, a finger curled into Daniel's palm as though it was a countdown to an explosion.

"My date will be here soon. You should leave," Deborah said.

"The man is a fool for keeping you waiting."

Daniel puffed up his chest and stood tall in front of the table. Glaring at the man, he said, "I believe you're in my seat."

The man's gaze ping–ponged from Daniel to Deborah, but he didn't budge.

Daniel leaned in and put one fist on the table, getting up close to the man. "You need to un–ass my chair."

"He was just leaving," Deborah said.

The man grabbed his drink and stood next to Daniel. He had youth on his side, but Daniel noticed he lacked in the height—as well as manners—department. He left the table, heading to the bar to possibly find another victim for the night.

Daniel scowled at the man until he'd walked a safe distance away. He then sat and looked at Deborah. "You all right?"

Deborah nodded. "Apparently, that man was never taught manners."

Speaking of manners, Daniel had arrived late. "I didn't mean to keep you waiting." Daniel felt bad for her having to deal with such a loser. "I didn't realize someone would be hitting on you."

"Men hit on women all the time, especially in bars. I was handling it."

"I didn't mean to imply that you weren't handling it. I'm just sorry you needed to." Did men hit on her all the time? He'd never thought of her going out on dates to bars, but it was possible.

Now that he sat close to her, he had a clear view of her plunging neckline. The woman must never go out in the sun because her flawless skin looked baby–smooth.

"Did you want to order a drink or something before we go?" she asked.

Good Lord, he was practically gawking at her so he quickly averted his eyes. Something about her was different tonight. She wore dresses all the time at work; although, not a dress like this. And her hair was normally neatly and professionally pulled back, not like it was tonight, all loose and sexy and framing her face.

He then realized what was missing. "Can you see without your glasses?" he asked, making sure to only look at her face.

"Contacts." Deborah took the last sip of her Sprite. "I've had them for years, but don't prefer them." She took a deep breath. "Caroline suggested I wear them."

Daniel remembered that the contract had mentioned a spa day so he pointed to her hair. "You look different."

Different? She looked gorgeous in a sundae—no, in a banana split—type of way. Stunning dress. Sexy body. His gaze once again moved to her ample bosom, which nearly popped out of the gown.

Her hand touched a brunette lock of hair. "Caroline suggested a new style, so…"

He glanced back up at her hairstyle. "You look beautiful." The bartender approached, but there was no time for drinks. Daniel stood and held out his arm. "Are you ready for dinner?"

Deborah felt like a fish out of water. Hopefully, no one could tell. This was only an elegant dinner out, so why was she sweating so much? She had eaten with Daniel in the past. Sure it was mainly food they had ordered into the office when they worked late, but this evening would be nothing different.

Mas Rafs' elegance and class impressed her, and they had only valeted the rental car and stood in front of the place. How many times had she confirmed dinner reservations at this location on Daniel's calendar?

Tonight her curiosity would be fulfilled. This restaurant's reputation preceded it, and it always received high marks from the food critics.

It was also expensive as hell.

She had just draped the stole higher on her shoulders and placed some dark glasses on to conceal her identity when Daniel held out the crook of his arm. "If you wouldn't mind."

A flush of embarrassment warmed her cheeks. This was a date. She needed to remember that. She was allowed, and expected, to touch the man. Her heart pounded as she entwined her arm with his. "Sorry, I should have… well, of course, sir."

A light flickering from across the parking lot caught her attention, even through her sunglasses. A photographer was taking their picture. She hadn't expected the show to begin this early, especially with a different rental car, but according to the contract, she needed to act like a loving fiancée.

Daniel kept walking as though he hadn't noticed

the man and his camera. She now leaned in to whisper about the photographer. Daniel's head jerked as though surprised she was standing so close to him. In a slightly louder voice than she had intended, she whispered, "The press is already here, darling."

She had wondered what, if any, endearing name she might call him. Many of the names she had considered didn't fit. And she would never embarrass him with a name such as Pookie and the like. Somehow 'darling' felt more appropriate.

His stature softened, and he did his part of pretending to be her love interest. "I had hoped that the picture Scott took in his office would be enough," Daniel said. "I guess the vultures just need more."

He held her closer in what felt a much more intimate way, which now allowed her to get a good whiff of his cologne. She knew exactly which brand he preferred since she kept his house stocked. The fragrance was a high–quality one with a light muskiness. She'd just never stood close enough to appreciate it before. The wind picked up, and she inhaled deeply, enjoying the scent.

Just before they entered the restaurant, several reporters called out Daniel's name, which proved that Caroline's tweet leakage to the media certainly paid off well. Maybe too well considering how many people were here.

Deborah knew this was the first time Daniel would be making a public appearance with her fiancée, but she had never been the attention of the paparazzi before. She didn't like the attention and now understood why Daniel hated it, and had always avoided it. Everyone in the crowd now stared at them and cameras and microphones were being thrust in their faces.

There were several questions, and they were jumbled together so that she couldn't make out one reporters voice over another.

The only sentence that did make its way through was a deep voice that stood out. It wasn't a question, just more of a demand for Daniel to give his fiancée a kiss.

Her mind had barely enough time to process the request before she felt him grasp her waist and pull her closer. She sucked in a deep breath a second before his lips touched hers.

His strong arm held her waist from behind, which was good since she felt her knees give way. The kiss was tender and chaste, but only one sided. She hadn't even moved her lips or… hell, he could have kissed a mannequin and gotten more of a response.

The kiss ended as quickly as it had started, and she looked away finding it hard to make eye contact with anyone.

Not that she had any right to do so, but how often had she dreamed about kissing Daniel? Decades? The moment was gone before it had even really begun. The kiss was flat and…and…her lips curled up in a smile. She had kissed Daniel! Oh, it wasn't a kiss that would ever make it into a romance novel, but the next one…

The next one would… Her fantasy began taking off. It'd be passionate, it'd be rich with emotion, it would… No, it needed to feel the same way. Flat and uneventful.

Too much was at stake.

She may be a key member in this little farce, but that was all it was. A fictitious story that needed to remain in la-la land.

There'd be no passion. There'd be no excitement. There'd be no invitation up to her room extended.

Nothing.

The crowd gave way now that they got what they wanted. They then entered the dimly lit restaurant, which oozed romance. His touch still lingered on her lips, so she touched them and told herself that the kiss meant nothing. This was a business agreement, and nothing else.

"Our table should be ready," he said.

A man dressed in a suit held up his arms, walked the entry's small hallway, and greeted them. He gave Daniel a half–handshake and half–hug greeting.

"Deborah, this is Adam. He owns the restaurant."

Adam Levinson, the owner of the place—and another person to perform in front of.

She took a deep breath and focused on the task at hand.

It was dinner.

Dinner out with Daniel at a fine restaurant.

She could do this.

She could have recognized Adam's voice anywhere since she had talked to him numerous times over the phone. Giving him a pleasant smile and extending her hand for a handshake, Deborah was surprised when he took the offering and gently kissed the back of her hand.

The man inspected her from head to toe and then a twinkle appeared in his eye. "This one is a keeper, Daniel."

Her jaw fell slack and she gaped at the man. She felt on display, and yet, all she could think of was the scene from Disney's *Lady and the Tramp* with the restaurant owner saying to Tramp, "You keepa dis one."

She hoped spaghetti wasn't going to be served.

"I set up a private room for you tonight, and I asked the chef to prepare something extra special." Adam gestured with his hand for them to follow. "I hope you like Italian."

An image of her and Daniel sharing a spaghetti noodle appeared in her mind. This was her boss, not her date. She planned to order the most expensive entrée. There would be no sharing of food tonight.

17

*A*ccording to the *Self-Made Diva* magazine, Daniel needed to practice how to connect with a woman on a date, and Ms. Baxter would be the perfect guinea pig. So why was he struggling to get the words out?

It was probably due to the kiss outside the restaurant.

He had thought it would feel like kissing a sister or other female relative, but it didn't.

The kiss wasn't passionate, but his heart was pounding when he reached in and claimed her lips. The entire event had unsettled him, which was why the kiss was only a peck on the lips.

He took a deep breath to relieve his tension. New clothes, new hairstyle, new role... but same Ms. Baxter.

The excitement he had felt was just because the newness of it all. Nothing else.

Employees are off-limits.

Period.

He looked down at his empty glass and then caught the waiter's attention. "I'll take another," he said, ordering his second scotch of the evening in a more aggravated tone than he had intended.

After having memorized the top five dinner conversation starters from his latest edition of *Self–Made Diva*, he leaned in and continued with question number four, hoping to get more of a conversation going than just a yes or no answer.

"What's your biggest fear, Deborah?"

Her widened eyes suggested that he had surprised her.

She glanced away. With a slight hint of a nervous smile and a shake of her head, she said, "Well, like you, probably a fear of security."

A five-word answer, nothing more. It was interesting that she shared that same fear.

"What kind of security?" he asked, prodding her for more information.

A distant look crossed her face, then a slight blush. "I didn't have a lot growing up. I had the love of a good family, but not much money."

A spark of hope kindled within him. He had asked the right question. He had always suspected as much since she mostly packed her lunches and, as far as he could tell, she never took extravagant vacations.

He wanted to keep the conversation going. "Your family didn't have much of life's little extras?"

She took a sip of her water. "Nothing such as extras. No. We were poor"—she glanced away but then made eye contact with him—"and I have an older sister. Sometimes,… we didn't even have enough food."

Her voice was soft with a whiff of sorrow.

She then paused as though deciding whether or not to continue sharing, but then she took a deep breath. "We always ate three meals a day, don't get me wrong, but I'd be hungry most nights. I would get free breakfast from the school district, but that was only during the school year. The summer months were the hardest, but the local area Food Bank would help us."

She smiled and waved off the last statement, but he suspected the story pained her deeply by the way her eyes were tearing up.

"I got a job in high school, which helped my family," she said. "Being the youngest, my money didn't have to help feed more than just my parents and me once Sue got a scholarship and went to college." Deborah took a deep breath. "My father got a promotion at work just as she left, so much of the money I earned helped me attend college."

He felt a wall being torn down between them, and he felt closer to her. "I'm so sorry, Deborah."

Dedicated, loyal, and hardworking. Those were three characteristics Daniel always associated with her, and now he knew why. They were instilled in her very early in life.

Her green eyes sparkled in the candlelight. She'd said she hated wearing contacts, but she looked amazing without glasses. Her hair was also more feminine and soft than he had ever seen it before. Some days, he figured her tight bun must give her headaches. Tonight, her hair flowed freely over her shoulders, brushing them softly as she turned her head or laughed.

"What do you do in your time off?" he asked, moving on to the next question—and hoping it was less painful for her.

"I like putting on comfortable blue jeans and a T-shirt and…well, I like going to quiet coffee houses and writing."

That's right. She had mentioned something about writing years ago to him. "Novels?"

She didn't answer. She only blushed, which made her look more radiant than ever before.

Enjoying the conversation, he felt drawn to her full, red lips. She even smiled throughout the evening. She never scowled around the office, but here, at this moment, she appeared happy. She had a smile that lit up the room.

Her lips also looked soft and kissable.

Staring into her eyes, and at those glorious lips,

kept him from focusing on her cleavage. Even wearing his jacket now since she had mentioned how cold the room felt, he still had a marvelous view of a great deal of flesh.

He pulled himself away and now focused his gaze on the bread and butter on the table.

What the hell was he doing?

This was a contractual dinner with an employee. An employee who only took this assignment to help *him* out. She had made it perfectly clear that nothing was to come between the two of them. The last thing he needed was to lose the best assistant he ever had, and possibly, get a law suit to deal with.

He was better than this.

"But enough about me." She poked the food and moved it around on her plate. "Tell me more about you."

He never shared too much of his stories with others, but he mentioned his hometown, she already knew he had been the star quarterback of his high school team. Of course, she had seen and taken care of his tenth and twentieth high school reunion invitations. He hadn't attended either of them, but not because of a lack of preparation. Deborah was more than willing to set up hotel reservations and flights for him. Instead, she sent out his regrets for not attending them.

"Before I forget," Deborah said, "please remember the company all–hands quarterly meeting is in one week. I've gathered the statistics from the five department heads and have begun the work on your presentation, but"—she shook her head—"I didn't have time to finish it."

And, as if by magic, his assistant Ms. Baxter returned—sans hair bun, glasses, and a business suit. He stared at Deborah, finding it hard to believe that this was the same woman who had shared his office for the past eighteen years.

The waitress appeared with their dessert. Daniel had known the young lady for years since she was Adam's daughter, but he'd never bothered to ask her anything about her life. Deborah had no issue with asking questions and getting to know the people around her. Thanks to Deborah's questions, they found out that the girl worked at the restaurant in the evenings and on the weekends while putting herself through school.

How did he not know that? He had thought her name was Teresa until Deborah read her nametag and began calling her Tessa.

Daniel downed his scotch.

He was paid to run businesses, not be a people person. There was no need to feel embarrassed... God, did he really call the girl by the wrong name for years? Had he done so in front of her father?

"Are you sure you'll be able to drive?" Deborah asked and then tasted her slice of cheesecake.

That's right. He'd driven tonight. Surely he shouldn't get behind the wheel.

"You can drive my car back to the hotel, that is if you don't mind. I'll take a cab back to my home."

"Do you think that's wise?"

He glanced at his empty glass. "I shouldn't be driving."

She shook her head. "If the photographers are still outside, won't it appear odd if we don't leave together?"

Deborah always thought ahead and took care of all the little details. It's why he relied so heavily on her.

"I'll leave my car, and Adam will see that it gets home," Daniel said. "We can take a cab back to your hotel, and then I'll have the driver take me home."

Exiting from the side door and into a cab would allow them to ditch any reporters outside. He wasn't going to stay the night with Deborah at the hotel, and he didn't want the reporters disturbing her privacy.

He bit his lip and focused on that single thought. He *wasn't* going to stay the night with Deborah. He swallowed the lump in his throat. He had to keep this arrangement professional and just remember that she was his assistant, not his date.

18

*D*aniel returned home, alone.

After securing the iron gate which lead onto his property, he pulled his car into the garage. Deborah had already texted that she had made it safely to her hotel suite without any press or notice by anyone.

She was safe and secure.

That meant a lot to him.

Oreo and Ginger welcomed him once he entered his home. Their tails wagged and they barked to greet him. They were great security guards, but more than that, they were faithful pets.

"Let me get the two of you some dinner. It's late."

They followed him into the kitchen where he refilled their bowls and made sure they had water. He then took them upstairs.

"We can watch some television tonight and cuddle." Entering his bathroom, he got ready for bed, noting that his jacket held the slight scent of Deborah's perfume. He was certain that she was already asleep, but he was tempted to call her. Call and just talk.

There were still some more conversational tips in the magazine he wanted to go over. But they'd have to wait until their next date.

Date.

No, their next 'business meeting'. He could practice the magazine tips then.

"I've got in over my head," he said to the dogs as he got into bed. He scooted Oreo aside but Ginger leaned in and licked his face repeatedly. Their normal bedtime routine.

"Okay. Okay," he said, laughing while Ginger licked him. "Candy kisses. Yum. Yum. Yum." He scratched her lower back. "Good girl."

When Ginger moved over to the other pillow on the bed and plopped down, Daniel scooted himself over to reach his other dog who lay at the foot of the bed. "The reporters were all over us at the restaurant." He patted Oreo's belly and looked deep into his soulful eyes. "Don't worry though. Deborah is fine. I'll make sure no one bothers her." After rubbing the dog's ears, which always calmed the puppy and got him to sleep, he said, "Good boy."

There wasn't much on television so he left it on for background noise. Instead of focusing on an old Cary Grant romance, he opened his phone's app and started scanning its articles.

"Dog or Cat? The Importance of Pets in a Relationship," one article read.

He smiled and scanned past the article to the next one.

Deborah loved dogs.

"Should You Keep Secrets from Your Lover," was another article.

"The answer to that one is no," he said to his dogs who had settled in and were nearly asleep on the bed.

"How to Enjoy Your Best Orgasm Ever," was a third article. He decided to read through that one. For being a man of nearly forty, the tips were not that surprising to him, but the article was written from a woman's point of view. What women wanted. What they expected. What they wished for.

If he could believe the article, women knew exactly what they wanted but didn't know how to tell their lover. The article contained links to follow up stories. One was about how to share your inner-most thoughts with the person you share a bed with.

He started reading the next article but found himself having to scan back and start it over again. His eyes drooped and he just needed to get some sleep.

In his dream, he sat in the backroom of a bar. The thick smell of alcohol and smoke filled his nostrils, and he could tell he was not alone. The faint scent of perfume lingered in the air, as well.

His mystery brunette joined him in the private room. Boxes filled the tiny space, and the door didn't lock. Anyone, at any time, could catch them.

She stood naked except for spiked high heels and a red sun hat, the kind that gardeners wore. By the way she tilted her head, he couldn't make out her face. Her dark, brunette curls hung loosely along her silhouetted face, and out of nowhere, she held a lipstick tube and applied the fire engine redness to her full lips.

She knelt in front of him and unzipped his pants. Tugging his cock through the opening, she freed his erection. It sprang forth, swollen and throbbing to be touched. His heart raced as he anticipated her tongue gliding up his manhood and her taking him deep into her mouth, allowing the red lipstick to stain him.

With his left hand, he grabbed hold of the windowsill for support as her warm tongue stroked a path up his shaft and she held his balls gently. He moaned as she swirled her tongue around the tip and slid him inside.

She moaned in delight as she closed her lips around his throbbing length, causing Daniel's stomach to tighten. She sucked enthusiastically, and he needed to grip the windowsill tighter as he thrust more firmly into her mouth.

With his free hand, he touched the top of her red, floppy hat to hold her head and guide her.

Just as his hand brushed against the hat, and he had a chance to maybe see her face, he woke up.

19

"What do you mean the article says I'm pregnant?" This type of drama shouldn't be allowed so early in the morning, and Deborah already regretted letting Caroline in the hotel suite.

She grabbed Caroline's phone from her hand and glared at the posting, studying the picture. "Do I look pregnant?"

Caroline gave a pfft sound. "Looks altered." She then made a Vanna White impersonation over her own belly. "*This* is a baby bump. Your waist is slender and trim. There's nothing you need to worry about."

She then studied Deborah's thin waist. "By the way, I hate you for your hourglass figure."

Deborah sighed and thought of the expression, "Don't shoot the messenger." She still wanted to scream at someone, but, instead, read the article—starting with the video.

She watched as Ellington left the baby store with the lone purchase in his cart. Pausing the video for a moment, she said, "Daniel hates to shop, and this explains why he was late last night to pick me up. This video was posted last night to this newsfeed. Did you take this video?"

"Me? No. I was out with Scott last night. Besides," she said, pointing to the video, "this looks like it was taken from a distance—and from someone's car. Any video I would have taken would be closer up. My bet is that the reporter was following Daniel last night."

"Are there any…?" Deborah began to ask.

"Reporters downstairs?" Caroline asked. "No. I guess Daniel gave them the slip before arriving at the hotel."

Deborah continued the video. Tilting her head, she read the description of the present from the side of the box. Immediately after doing so, she gazed over to Caroline. "I don't think his gift to you and Scott is a surprise any longer. Sorry."

Caroline waved her hand dismissively as though that was the least of their worries. "It's the thought that counts. Keep watching."

Deborah broke out in a fit of laughter as she watched Daniel struggling with the box to stow it in the trunk. Daniel always had an air of decorum about him, and the suit he wore made the video just that much more fun to watch. Swearing and slamming the trunk shut was so unlike him.

"The funniest part about this," Deborah said, "is that I already bought his gift for you. And, to make it ironic, I got this exact security system. It's being delivered the day of your shower."

"We own a big house, I'm sure we can make use of both gifts." Caroline gave a wry smile. "The hashtag #EllingtonSecretBaby is trending right now. Most other news sites aren't showing the funny video, just rumoring that a baby is on its way."

Just like the proverbial feather pillow being ripped open atop a mountain, lies were hard to keep. Once the feathers flew everywhere, especially in a breeze, it became an impossible task to gather them once again.

Deborah understood that there was no way to undo what had already been done. "This rumor will die soon enough. People will either realize they have their own lives to worry about and stop listening to these crazy stories, or the lack of a baby will shut them up."

It then occurred to her. "Has Daniel seen this video?"

Caroline shook her head. "He's not much into social media, but he has to have heard about it by now." She crossed the room and held Deborah's hand. "Tonight, the two of you are going to the opera."

Caroline took her phone back and placed it in her pocket. "Do you like opera?"

Deborah glared at her friend. It wasn't the stupidest question, but, at what these tickets cost, it wasn't as though Deborah could afford such extravagance. Since Caroline had worked as a waitress for years, she understood the financial challenges.

"Yeah, I heard it once I'd said it." Caroline walked to the closet and inspected the outfits. "You may want to wear something comfortable."

"Why is that?"

"If you're like me, you'll be asleep long before intermission." Caroline inspected each gown before moving it aside. "You've already worn the nicest gown I loaned you. I think we should go shopping."

Deborah crossed the room and grabbed the first outfit she could reach in the closet. "There's no need to spend money. I'm sure this will be all right."

Caroline touched the taffeta fabric. "This one is lovely. If it were me, though, I'd go with a sleek design to show the absence of a baby bump... but, if you want all this excess material across your midriff..."

Good point. The press didn't need any encouragement. She didn't enjoy spending money, and hoped Daniel was having a better day than she was. "Let's go shopping."

Daniel's bad day just got worse.

"He's drop–dead gorgeous," Suzy Ortiz whispered into her office phone. "You'd never expect an old geezer like him to be this handsome. Naturally, he has the charm of an overbearing professor, but I'm sure his money makes up a lot for his personality." She giggled and added, "Guess what? He's taking me on a business trip tomorrow."

How could the silly temp employee not notice him standing ten feet from her? Daniel didn't wear much cologne to announce his presence in a room, not like Ms. Ortiz and the swill of a perfume bottle she wore, but still.

He absolutely didn't want to take her on this trip, but the temp agency couldn't find a replacement in time.

"Get off the phone, Ms. Ortiz." His commanding voice echoed through the room, causing her to immediately hang up.

"What do you need?" Suzy asked, still lounging in the chair and swiveling back and forth.

She didn't say, "sir" to him, she didn't sit up in the chair, she didn't look interested in doing her job. He'd just finished a two–hour meeting, and, with the nauseous smell lingering in the air, he suspected all she'd managed to do was paint her nails and talk on the phone.

"I need you to do your job." He walked around the desk to where a Rolodex sat. The device was old school charm, but so was Ms. Baxter.

His finger paused on the dial. Deborah. *Deborah* was old school.

He flipped through the cards. There needed to be professional decorum between a boss and his assistant, but when Deborah returned, he wanted to call her by her first name. After all these years, and with him truly missing the way she ran the office, he no longer wanted the barrier of using last names between them.

He found the three cards he needed and pulled them from the roller. "We fly out in the morning."

"You already told me that." She sat straighter in the chair and leaned over. Her see–through blouse and push–up bra didn't impress him.

"I'll confirm all the reservations and pick up my dry cleaning." He held up his hand and indicated two of the three business cards. He held onto the third card because it was for a different temp agency.

He didn't have much time, and he knew he couldn't trust Ms. Ortiz to take care of the trip details and his packing. Plus, he didn't want her to pick up his dry cleaning and drop it off at his house while he was out with Deborah. Ms. Ortiz didn't need to know where he lived, and he certainly wasn't going to give her a key to his home and the guest security code.

He paused at the door. "It's a four–day trip."

"Uh huh. I know." She pointed to her phone. "It's programmed into my calendar app."

His eyes narrowed in on her. "We'll be meeting with Carl Weston, one of the company's founders, to discuss the upcoming year and do the yearly report for the company."

"Ellington–Weston," Her face lit up to what Daniel could only believe was a low watt bulb. Removing a pen from her desk, she wrote Carl Weston's name on her hand. "I'm making a note of that."

Deep down in his gut he knew he'd have to say his next sentence. "Please pack business appropriate clothing."

She did a cursory glance at her outfit and then said in a mocking tone, "Of course, sir."

The words sent a chill down his spine. Deborah said them with respect. Ms. Ortiz's tone held only sarcasm.

He walked to the door. "And remember to turn off the lights and put the outside phone lines into nighttime mode."

God, what else did he have to do?

That's right. He needed her phone number so he could reach her while they were in Los Angeles. "What's your number?" he asked.

She gave him what he suspected to be a seductive look—which only made her appear constipated—and rambled off her digits. At the very least, he could now contact her if needed. In fact, he hated that he had to do this, but he quickly Googled, "what to wear on a business trip," and texted her the link. "You now have my number, as well."

She licked her lips. "You can call me anytime, day or night, Daniel."

He glared at her. "There will never be anything between us. My secretary will return soon, and you will be of here, with no one missing you."

Her face hardened and she turned her back to him.

Like he cared. If he had his way, the temp agency would send someone else to attend this trip with him. Anyone but Goldilocks.

Just as he was about to pocket his phone, his *Self–Made Diva* app displayed the number fifty–six, showing that he was behind in the newsfeed, so he opened it and read the first notice.

His knees weakened and he thought he'd collapse to the floor.

Now there was a baby? He gulped some air and just wanted to scream. How on earth did he go from having a fake fiancée to being a fake father–to–be? The press needed to write books because this line of fantasy would sell millions.

"Is there anything else you need?"

From her? No. "Don't show up late at the airport," he said and then he stormed out of the office.

Several of the postings contained pictures of him and Deborah out last night. There were arrows drawn, pointing to her belly. The label being "*baby bump.*"

She couldn't be pregnant. He assumed the articles were vicious gossip until he saw one picture where the fabric of the dress bunched around her waist.

Was she pregnant?

He walked down the hallway to the elevator, putting the phone away. People passed him in the corridor but he just kept walking. He reached the elevator before he realized it.

She hadn't drunk last night, but had merely claimed she didn't drink alcohol. She'd also postponed a date so she could fulfill the contract he'd had her sign.

Her eagerness to sign the contract once he'd mentioned that he'd pay her now made more sense. She'd come from humble beginnings, raised a child on her own, and was now pregnant and alone once again. His Deborah needed money for the baby.

20

*D*eborah sat straighter in her plush auditorium box seat at the opera and listened to the aria, trying hard to stifle a yawn. Caroline was wrong. Comfortable clothing was not the way to go. She should have worn something to keep her awake, even if it meant uncomfortable shoes.

The performance of *Tristan and Isolde* enthralled Daniel. He'd even commented that it was one of his favorite operas. He hadn't taken his eyes off the screen since the performance started. He seemed so happy, so at peace. The tension lines that normally creased his forehead were gone, as was the hardened chin and jaw he had during the day when dealing with the business. Right now, he looked comfortable.

She had to admit, she watched more of him that of the opera itself. Two people screaming in German.

Not her thing, although, she could figure out the gist of the story.

The character Isolde pretended to be a handmaiden, won the heart of a brave warrior who believed her station to be beneath him, and then she married another man, whom she did care for. Two fantastic, heroic, and wealthy men fighting over one woman.

How unrealistic.

In her experience, many men still didn't want to be married. It didn't matter if they had been dating you for years, or even after you told them there was a baby on the way.

Which explained why people enjoyed this story. It was fantasy, not real world.

"Would you like a glass of wine?" Daniel leaned in and whispered. His hand gestured to the fruit and cheese platter they had ordered.

A glass of wine would complement it perfectly, and although she did enjoy a glass occasionally, she never drank in mixed company.

She shook her head. "No, thank you." Her coffee cup was nearly empty so she reached down to pick it up. The engagement ring clanked against the porcelain mug. She was certain no one heard the noise, but she was aware of the ring every time she touched anything.

The dimness of the opera hall lights didn't allow the facets of the diamond to pick up any light and cast reflections, but she had noticed them while shopping earlier in the day, while getting ready for the evening, and in the car when the diamond had caught the last few rays of the setting sun.

She took a deep breath. She didn't want to think about the ring, or that it meant nothing between her and Daniel. She downed her remaining bit of coffee. The caffeine would keep her up all night, but she was sure this opera would have her out in no time.

"Are you drinking decaf?"

"What?" Deborah leaned in, her head mere inches from his, allowing her to smell his musky cologne even more. With this being the closest thing to a date she had been on in ages, she realized she missed going out. Perhaps the man Caroline had selected for the blind date, whoever he was, would stir her as much as Daniel did. At the very least, he could be a distraction.

Daniel nodded toward the coffee cup in her hands.

"I'm fine," she finally said. Why the interest in what she drank? She glanced at her watch. It would soon be intermission. Now his concern made sense.

Deborah focused her attention to the opera, but she noticed Daniel oddly staring at her. His gaze sent shivers down her spine, and in all the right—or *wrong* depending on how you looked at it—ways, so she refocused on something else. The last thing she needed was to fantasize about her boss.

Although he did look amazing in his tux. His face

held just enough scruff from the lack of a shave to drive any woman crazy, and his hair was perfectly tousled—perfect to run your hand through.

She placed the empty coffee cup down and decided to concentrate on something that would keep her attention. The boxed seat and the hall were a perfect choice.

She studied the area and took note of the height and how the layout of the room below looked from this perspective. Her latest book release was out, and she needed a fresh idea for novel number three.

Her lips curled upward in a big smile. Her first book was more of a novella and not a very good one at that. But book number two was her masterpiece. She had worked on it for five years, with many revisions and second–guessing of what the ending would be.

The sales were not impressive, but the book was only her second release. She'd initially called it *Loving Him*, but the title sounded like a Christian's relationship with God. She'd finally settled on the name, *Of Course, Sir*. The book cover's image held a secretary dressed in a red gown, placing her hand on the chest of a man wearing a tuxedo. His face wasn't in view of the image, allowing readers to mentally dream up what the hero of the story looked like.

In her mind, the hero looked exactly like Daniel. In particular, the way he looked tonight. She had already planned to buy a red dress for the evening, but it wasn't until Caroline had seen this one hanging in the store that she'd insisted Deborah buy it.

Novel number two didn't contain a sexy opera scene, but perhaps novel number three might. The red velvet curtains on the wall, and the gold trim accents exuded much elegance. She enjoyed the warm, romantic glow, which the sconces and chandeliers cast across the entire auditorium. The musicians, tightly packed into the musical pit below, created a rich sound that had the walls vibrating.

But the box seat felt more intimate. It held six chairs, but they weren't tethered to the ground, allowing you to arrange them any way you'd like.

She figured Daniel had bought out the small area to give them privacy. They wouldn't need to put on a show if they were the only people up this high.

Yawning once more, she found it difficult to keep her eyes open. She leaned back in the chair, opened her eyes wide, and stared at the performance below.

That's when she felt his arm around her bare shoulders.

"Are you cold?"

Before she could answer, Daniel removed his tux jacket. She leaned forward so he could drape it around her. The scent of his cologne enveloped her. She breathed in deeply, enjoying the sudden sensation of his body warmth from the jacket.

His hand lingered on the fabric and then finally

made its way up to her cheek. He caressed her face and gazed into her eyes. "I can keep you warm."

The music suddenly stopped, and the room grew darker, giving them perfect privacy. He stared at her lips and then glanced back up to her eyes.

"I've wanted you for a long time, Deborah."

Leaning in, he kissed her. His fingers tangled in her hair as he pulled her closer to him. He lifted her effortlessly and put her in his lap. His one free hand knocked her chair down and it tumbled to the floor.

Glancing around, she figured no one had heard the noise. It was hard to tell since the box set railing now blocked her view from everything else in the hall. Everything that is except Daniel's piercing blue eyes. They were filled with desire.

Desire for her.

The fabric of the dress caught beneath her, but only for a minute. Daniel stood and moved the other chairs, giving them the center of the floor. He then placed his hand under her bottom and scooped her to the middle of the space, laying her on the carpet.

She felt the heat pooling in her core and dripping to her panties. She was going to make love to Daniel. After all these years, *he* wanted *her*.

Her heart pounded with excitement, and the need to have him grew, especially when he pulled up the skirt of her dress, grabbed her lace panties and ripped the fabric off her. She now lay open and revealed to him.

Placing her foot atop one of the chairs, she tilted her hips in anticipation. He barely undid his pants before he lay on top of her.

There was no hesitation.

His throbbing shaft dove into her wet folds, her body wanting him and hugging him intimately as he pumped into her.

It was dirty sex. Dirty on the floor sex.

Good dirty on the floor sex.

She hoisted her legs up higher, not caring if the people down below could see her foot moving in time with the rhythmic touch that was driving her crazy.

Just as she was about to cry out, a buzzing noise woke her. She then noticed the lights flickering above her.

"It's intermission," Daniel said. "Let's stretch our legs and get more refreshments."

She scanned the room. The remaining four chairs remained where they had been earlier in the evening, and Daniel still wore his tux jacket. It had all been a dream.

A dream she would never forget, especially since she planned to put an opera scene in her next novel.

21

*D*eborah drew open the curtains of her hotel room window and let in the morning light. Her room was on the highest floor and she glanced to the parking lot below.

Had a member of the press followed her home last night? She couldn't see any camera crews or news vans below, so maybe her imagination was getting the best of her.

She needed to stop being paranoid.

The catnap during the opera had acted as a wake–up call, one she didn't care for. She didn't need to alter her relationship with her boss. It needed to remain professional, even if she had wanted to invite him into her hotel room last night.

Thank goodness she'd come to her senses. Of course, Daniel had needed to leave early for a flight this morning so there couldn't have been any festivities after the opera anyway.

Daniel would be gone for the next four days. The time apart would give her some perspective and a chance to reflect on her utter stupidity.

Last night's dress had been a mistake, one she would not make again. She lived in reality, not in one of the scenes from her books.

Caroline had insisted that she buy the red, beaded dress with spaghetti straps and a plunging neckline the moment she'd seen it in the store. Caroline couldn't have known, but the outfit matched the one the heroine in Deborah's last novel wore to an art gala with her boss where she pretended to be his date for the evening.

Deborah paused and realized she had begun pacing the room.

Had Caroline read her novel?

Thinking back, her book also contained the scene from Mas Rafs the first night. A dark, intimate room at a five–star restaurant where they dined…well, in the book, heated sex atop the table occurred. That certainly hadn't happened with her and Daniel in real life.

She shook her head. Daniel loved Mas Rafs, which was why the restaurant had made its way into her novel. There was nothing amiss here with Caroline. After all, Deborah wrote under a pen name to hide her identity for that very reason. Caroline couldn't have known about the scenes from her book.

Crossing the room, she stretched and woke herself up. Rarely did she have any time off, and with Daniel out of town for a few days, she truly had nothing better to do than work on her next novel.

The hero was a wealthy boss, just like in her first book, but this one falls in love with his secretary. Deborah sat at the desk in the room and typed away, filling in an opera scene since the imagery remained fresh in her mind.

The dream last night had ended abruptly, but that wouldn't be the case in her book. She'd make sure the main characters ended up lying entwined together on the floor of the opera house's box seat, with the music playing on and rising to a crescendo just as the two climaxed.

She scrolled the text up on her computer to the top of the scene and slowly read it once more, editing it here and there for spicier words like, "undulate," "throbbing," and "desperation."

The scene scorched the page, in all the right ways. She crossed her legs repeatedly as she read it a second and then a third time.

She mentally gave herself a high-five. This was five–out–of–five star rating of good writing.

A slight tinge of disappointment washed over her. Fantasy lived in an entirely different world, and she had never had such an explosive love making session in her life.

Daniel didn't place his jacket on her last night, didn't hold her throughout the performance, and didn't kiss her good night—or anything else—before saying goodbye to her. Which was exactly what she'd expected.

A part of her felt disappointed to not be attending the conference in Los Angeles with him. This was the first trip since Josh had left for college that Deborah could have gone on without worrying about her son and leaving him at her sister's house for days.

It would have been her first business trip with Daniel where she didn't have to worry about what was going on at home. But she was here instead, and Daniel was on the trip with his temporary secretary. Deborah was certain the new hire was young and attractive. Being a temp was also an added appeal for Daniel. There were no lingering goodbyes to deal with.

Just a four-day, fun-filled, five-star hotel stay with a hot, young woman eager to do whatever he wanted. The two of them were probably alone in his plane right now, maybe making it into the 'mile high' club.

Deborah shook her head and took in a deep breath. She needed to call Caroline and go out. Sitting in this room alone and writing sex scenes all day long while she thought of Daniel off with his young, temp secretary was going to drive her mad.

"I thought you weren't going to attend the," Daniel said, pausing to think of the name, "the brain surgery numb-a-thon conference I believe you called it."

"Neurosurgery Symposium." Ravi shifted in his seat and looked out the private Ellington-Weston plane on the tarmac. "I changed my mind since the weather is nice. Thanks for the last-minute lift."

The flight attendant walked up the aisle of the small six-seater plane. "Mr. Ellington." She placed a scotch on the table in front of Daniel.

Ravi caught the woman's attention. "Honey, I'd like the same."

The woman glared at Ravi. "Life is filled with disappointments, Ravi." Her voice was spiked with hatred, causing Daniel to sternly look over to his employee.

"Sorry, Mr. Ellington." Her face turned red as though she had temporarily lost herself in the moment. "Another scotch coming up."

"Angela, I thought that was you." Ravi plastered the fake smile on his face he usually wore when he got caught in a compromising situation, but Angela ignored him and walked back to the galley.

"You read her nametag, didn't you?"

"Was it obvious?"

Daniel glanced at his watch and then stared at the

entrance of the plane. "I think Angela remembers you."

"What did I ever do to her?"

"You forget, this isn't the first time you've flown on my plane. You probably never called her back."

Ravi's eyes narrowed and he sank into his seat. "This trip will be shitty. She'll probably spit in my scotch."

Daniel's eyes widened and he shook his head. "I sure the hell wouldn't drink it."

A young man walked onto the plane, his off-the-rack suit a bit too big and a bag with a computer swinging from his shoulder.

"I'm sorry I'm late, sir."

"You're right on time." Daniel gestured to the man. "This is my new hire in advertising, Evan."

Evan shook Ravi's hand and then took a seat across the aisle from Daniel. "Thank you again sir for this great opportunity."

"I'm sure you'll make the company proud." Daniel shared with Ravi how he discovered his new marketing talent, emphasizing how studious Evan was when driving people around. He even mentioned, but didn't go into any detail, about how Evan was good at reading people—which was always an asset when it came to advertising.

Angela arrived with a half-empty scotch glass. "Enjoy, Ravi." She glanced over to Evan. "Sir, would you care for a beverage?"

"Yes, ma'am. A soda would be nice, if it isn't too much trouble."

Polite, courteous… the world was going to eat Evan alive. Daniel wanted to make the young man his pet project. He wanted to make sure he had a fair shake at a stellar career.

Ravi moved his drink away from his seat the second Angela left.

"Sir, shouldn't we have left ten minutes ago?" Evan asked.

Daniel checked his watch. If Ms. Ortiz wasn't here in the next two minutes, they would take off without her.

"I'm here," a shrilly voice sounded from the front of the plane.

Ms. Ortiz entered, plopped her coat and oversized purse down, and let out a groan. "I had to take two shuttles to get to this concourse. I'm lucky to have gotten here on time."

"Technically, you were late." Daniel pushed a button on his chair and signaled for Angela that they could take off.

"Please, sit here," Ravi said, gesturing to the seat in front of him which faced him. "You must be Daniel's new secretary."

A skeptical eye inspected both Evan and Ravi, and then Ms. Ortiz decided to take Ravi up on his offer. She puffed up her chest, took her seat, and her mini skirt rode up.

"I'm Dr. Ravi Amarro."

Her overly plastered smile showed her lipstick stained teeth. "I'm pleased to meet you, doctor. What's your specialty?"

The plane taxied and Daniel didn't enjoy the show. Ravi had hit on plenty of women in his day, and usually Daniel had no issues. But how hard up would he have to be to fall into Ms. Ortiz's traps?

Ravi began telling a boring surgical story, one that was filled with medical terms and sheer boredom. At times, Daniel thought the story even bored Ravi since he kept texting something on his phone.

A cackling giggle escaped Ms. Ortiz's mouth, and Daniel could tell she only pretended to be interested.

"Sir?" Evan asked, once he finished his soda. "When we arrive, I know you'll be meeting with your father and other board members."

Daniel held out his hand and stopped Evan. "My father can't come this year."

"Oh, sorry." Evan looked down at his laptop, still in the carry on. "I read that he'd be on the agenda. I hope everything is all right."

It was sweet to see the concern in Evan's eyes. "A minor medical issue. Nothing more. He'll visit the Chicago office soon and catch up."

After some chatter with Evan, a quick review of a few files, and an occasional node to Ravi, Daniel realized Ms. Ortiz had monopolized most of Ravi's attention during the trip—and the plane was scheduled to land in thirty minutes.

"If you'll excuse me, I'm going to freshen up." Ms. Ortiz stood and in a non-graceful manner fell into Ravi's lap.

"My goodness, the turbulence is so bad."

Evan leaned toward Daniel. "I didn't feel any…"

Daniel's hand rose. "No. Just let it go."

"A beautiful woman like you needs to be careful." Ravi helped her up and she walked to the back of the plane to find the bathroom.

Ravi's gaze followed her all the way down the short aisle. "Are you interested in her?" he asked Daniel once she was out of earshot.

Was he interested? You couldn't pay him enough to fall prey to a woman like her. "I'd rather keep my dignity."

Ravi glanced at the closed bathroom door. "Young. Beautiful. Energetic." He nodded his head in approval. "She's worth a few days of my time. I need to make this conference a little fun." He gave Evan a cursory glance. "You interested in her?"

Evan held up his hand and showed his wedding band, his face turning beet red in color. He leaned in so he was closer to Daniel. "Ms. Ortiz," he said, pointing to the back of the plane and whispering, "Is a single scoop of vanilla ice cream."

"I'm going to see if the lovely lady needs any help

in there." Ravi stood, loosened his tie, and walked to the back of the plane.

Evan watched as Ravi entered the bathroom. "Correction. A drippy single scoop of vanilla ice cream, no cone, that's fallen on the sidewalk with an anthill nearby."

22

*L*unch out. Now that was a great idea.

Deborah could be herself. No fake persona. No fake name. No fake anything.

Since Daniel was on the company jet flying to the conference, she figured the press would be following him, but she still wanted to play it safe. She dressed down in a soft t-shirt and comfy jeans. To complete the ensemble, she wore Jackie-O type of sunglasses to hide her face so she could make her way to the Ellington-Weston building without the media attacking her.

It had been a week, and the familiar hallways, faces, and noises beckoned to her as she made her way to Scott's office.

His door was ajar and she heard Caroline's familiar voice. Deborah checked her watch. She was right on time.

"You picked a winner," Caroline's voice drifted out to the hallway. "I don't even want to know where you found her."

"A little green goes a long way," Scott said. "If a client didn't pick her up, they were going to fire her. It was practically a mercy hiring."

Deborah knocked on the door and it opened. "May I come in?"

Caroline glanced at her watch. "Sorry. I lost track of time." She grabbed her jacket and stood, her free hand helping her off the chair.

"Who's a winner?" Deborah helped Caroline on with her coat.

Caroline's gaze darted to Scott; her jaw open as if she had been caught in a secret.

"Nannies," he quickly said. "We're thinking of hiring some care with the baby. You know,… especially at the beginning when we need to adjust to…"

Scott's phone beeped and he paused and glanced down at it, leaving an odd silence in the room.

Deborah focused on Caroline. "I thought you were against the idea of a nanny."

Caroline cocked her head to the side and glanced past Deborah, not making eye contact. "I'm keeping my mind open."

Scott laughed and set his phone down. When the ladies stared at him, he added, "I just got a funny text. It's nothing."

Caroline walked toward the door. "Have you heard from Daniel since he took off this morning?"

"He's still in the air." Deborah noticed an odd smile from Caroline aimed at Scott, who stifled a grin. "Is there something funny?"

Scott shook his head. "Ravi is paying off an old debt to me. Let's just say he isn't enjoying the task, that's all."

"Let's go, Deborah." Caroline stood at the now opened door.

Scott gave a dismissive wave and sat back at his desk. "Have a good lunch you two."

Deborah didn't know what she'd do if it wasn't for her good friend Caroline.

Four days of shopping, visiting a spa, going out to lunch with Caroline, and basically doing nothing productive... The boredom drove Deborah crazy, but at least she had company. And, it kept her mind off Daniel and the conference.

She quietly typed on her laptop while Caroline slept on the bed across the room in the luxurious hotel suite. Deborah found it difficult to focus on her story since Daniel was the inspiration, and he wouldn't be back in town for at least another hour.

Had it really been four full days since she'd last seen him?

Naturally, during holidays and vacations, she would not see him for this long, but he had attended an important business trip. She should have been with him. Not that she particularly cared for all the executives Daniel had met with.

Nearly nineteen years had passed, and she still couldn't face the founder of the company, the father of Josh. The man walked around these yearly meetings as though he hoarded all the oxygen in the room and everyone needed him for a hit.

Commanding, handsome, powerful,… regretful.

She took a deep breath and let it out slowly. He may be many things, but to her, he'd always be her one mistake. True, Josh had resulted from their one–night stand, and she'd never regret having him, but the bastard who fathered him could go straight to hell.

A tear threatened to roll down Deborah's cheek, and she mentally chided herself for the weakness. She had been all of twenty years old then, not even legally able to drink when she'd accepted his offer to the cocktail party. She'd been thrilled he had taken an interest in her and wanted her as his assistant, she just hadn't realized that getting drunk and being taken advantage of were part of his plan for her.

The alcohol had certainly made her willing that night. The company had recently gone public, the celebration was extensive, and she'd become a stupid, giddy girl. One who didn't think of any consequences.

She'd certainly thought of them the next day, and

especially two weeks later when she'd read the plus sign on the plastic stick.

He had ignored her afterward, moving on to the next woman in his parade of self–indulgence that his wife seemed to ignore. Did having so much money make you blind to your husband's dalliances? Or did she really not care?

The bastard had denied the baby and dismissed her from her position on some made–up disciplinary measures. Thinking back, Deborah should have sued the company, but she didn't want her mistake known.

Thankfully a job in a secretarial pool opened up. Less status, but equal pay. She would have quit and moved on if Daniel hadn't selected her from the secretarial pool as his personal assistant and secretary. Being eight months pregnant, Deborah knew she'd gotten the job based on her capabilities and skills, not her figure.

The nice raise she'd received by accepting the offer had allowed her to provide for her son.

Caroline stirred in the bed, but continued to snore, so Deborah checked her emails.

No word from Daniel. He would be back in Chicago within the hour, but she hadn't heard anything from him the entire time, and she suspected the temp secretary had kept him busy in the evenings.

Her body stiffened. Daniel was away from the press of Chicago, so there were less eyes to see him playing around behind his fake fiancée's back.

Deborah didn't want to think of the young, temp secretary sitting at her desk all week, seated next to Daniel on the plane, or anything else she may have been doing with the man during the conference. She was probably blonde and under thirty. Chances were, there was a parting gift for her in Deborah's desk drawer.

What was the going price these days? A diamond tennis bracelet for six months of attention? So a week of temp work would be…what? A gold bracelet?

Some bling and the door hitting you on your naked ass as he slammed it shut.

No office romance was worth it.

They never ended well, and they weren't worth the heartache.

Her heart pounded when her cell phone buzzed with a text. The noise startled her, and she didn't want it to wake Caroline, but more importantly, the text came from Daniel.

She scanned the message. Flew out early. Important meetings. Ellington–Weston planned to buy another company... Huh. He didn't mention which one, only that he had to work on a proposal all night and meet with the company lawyer in the morning. He asked her to set up a meeting with Scott to come over and help him with the pitch tonight.

A merger coming up, and now the purchase of a company? The man must be swamped.

Her gaze darted to Caroline, who still lay sleeping

on the bed. She understood just how tired a pregnant woman could be, but it wasn't as though she had any other plans this evening.

She texted back, "*Of course, sir.*"

23

*D*eborah drove to Daniel's estate and pushed the security buttons. The wind came in through the cracked window, chilling the interior of the car, as she waited for the gates to open, allowing her to drive down the pathway to Daniel's home. She felt as though she had been followed, but dismissed the idea since the iron gate would keep everyone out.

Being the center of media attention felt odd. The thought of someone taking her picture and posting that she was pregnant made her paranoid as to who could be lurking about.

Working out in the hotel gym the last few days and laying off carbs had given her a sense of accomplishment. Even though she told herself repeatedly that she didn't care what the media said, deep down, she did. And that bothered her since she had always taken pride in her figure and appearance.

She parked her car in the circular driveway and felt odd getting out of the vehicle, and then she realized why. She usually carried in dry cleaning, groceries, or some other item he needed her to bring over. Today, she brought in only her purse.

She paused and caught her reflection in the side mirror. She wasn't expecting to see him today, at least, not yet. Her disheveled hair and sparse makeup gave her a dressed down appearance. Instead of her crisp business suit, she wore a comfortable pair of jeans and a T–shirt. She gazed at her unbuttoned coat and saw the shirt peeking out.

Geez. There was a stain.

So much for taking pride in how she looked.

There was nothing she could do. Brushing away at the proof that she had eaten a gluten–free pizza for lunch, she realized the last time he'd seen her, she had been wearing a slim, fitted, red gown. If there had been anything between the two of them, the ugly ensemble she wore today would squash that.

Her horrible outfit may just be the perfect remedy. She was here to roll up her sleeves and get to work— not be on a date.

She marched down the walkway to the front door, and the motion sensor lights caught her presence. This visit was business. And that's all it will ever be. She wouldn't be foolish to fall for another boss. Never again.

Good Lord, Daniel needed help.

He sat at the kitchen table surrounded by paperwork. Electrical cords lay on the floor plugged into extension cables allowing him to keep two laptops running.

This second merger had been dropped in his lap. He knew their rival in the industry struggled to keep up, and buying them out and gaining their employees and company secrets was a huge win for Ellington–Weston.

So why could he only focus on Deborah? He glanced at the clock. She should be here by now.

The last time they had bought a rival security company, Deborah had helped him design the proposal. Daniel used that one as a template for this new merger, but Deborah seemed to have more finesse with such details.

She was needed in so many ways.

So many ways.

The doorbell rang, causing his two Shelties to wake from their nap and be on bark patrol. The noise became nearly deafening and he checked the monitor and saw Deborah standing outside.

She was here.

His jacket was off, so he made sure his shirt was tucked in. He grazed his hand over his hair and took a deep breath.

He opened the door and an explosion of fur nearly knocked him down.

"Hi, babies." She took timid steps trying to get in the door without stepping on paws or tails.

"Dammit. Watch out... Ginger peed."

Deborah side stepped the urine which had pooled in one area, but the dog's excitement had spread it across several of the marble tiles. Her brother, Oreo, was now taking an interest in it and smelling around the foyer. "Come babies. Outside."

Daniel worried about what to wear, what to say, what to do when he saw her again. Cleaning up dog pee was far from the list he had prepared, but it gave him something to do.

"They're excited to see you."

A heaviness lifted from his chest, and his lips spread into a huge smile. They weren't the only ones who'd missed her. Having her in the house was like a breath of fresh air.

Deborah glanced around once both dogs were out the now opened doggie door. "Are we the only ones here?"

"Yes." He disposed of the paper towel and washed his hands.

She placed her purse down on the kitchen counter. "I thought the temp secretary would be helping you."

Her voice sounded frosty, in a 'will I be disturbing the two of you' kind of way. He didn't like the tone but considering how many women he had been with over the years—how many that he had flaunted in front of Deborah—he could understand her coldness.

A syrupy feeling of shame covered him. Deborah had organized his dating life for years, a duty no personal assistant should have to do for her boss. "Ms. Ortiz…," he began, shaking his head.

Deborah's hand went up, she shook her head and didn't make eye contact. "You don't have to explain anything, Mr. Ellington."

He watched as she dug her glasses out from her purse, her body stiff, her lips pursed. She appeared hurt, perhaps even uncomfortable, by the mention of the temp. "She is the worst secretary I've ever worked with," he said, knowing that the woman's office skills were not what Deborah was focusing on.

"I hate her company. She is incompetent, intrusive, and just in the way." He shrugged and let out a deep breath. "Her intitled demeanor irritates me, and I can't wait to have you back."

Deborah's eyes lit up by the description. Daniel had many pet peeves, but an invasive person getting in Daniel's way was high on the list of people he avoided, and she knew it. "I'm sorry you've been struggling at the office in my absence."

"I need you to come back."

An awkward silence filled the room, but, at the very least, Deborah no longer looked uncomfortable. He gestured to the couch and the table covered with paperwork. "We should probably get to work."

Once settled and the work began, he said, "Have you seen the signed affidavit involving the contractors?"

Deborah remained busy scanning documents. She didn't even glance up but handed the requested file to Daniel. "Of course, sir."

He reached over, causing the books and paperwork between them on the couch to tumble. Without skipping a beat, Deborah straightened the mess before it fell to the floor.

The affidavit wrinkled in Daniel's hands, making a slight crunching noise since he had forcibly grabbed it from her as she'd dove to save the paperwork between them.

"No harm done." She read a file on her computer screen and her face pinched in a I'm-doing-a-hard-math-problem sort of way.

"Something wrong?"

She looked away from her laptop and set the paperwork down. "I just don't understand all this legal stuff." She stretched her arms and allowed her shoulder to pop from tension. "Legal documents always confuse me."

Grinning, he thought that they worked well together, like a pair of conjoined twins figure skating and winning gold. She understood the business and was always thorough in her work, even if she often misunderstood what the legal stuff was about.

"Scott will review everything in the morning. We

just need to focus on the takeover and warehouse supplies tonight."

His tie felt as if it were strangling him. He had already taken off his jacket, but he now removed the cursed noose and tossed it on the coffee table. "Can you read back the latest requirement involving liquidating all surplus and antiquated assets?"

"Of course, sir."

As she read back the proposal, he studied her as though seeing her for the first time. Her new hairstyle certainly complemented her face, but tonight it was pulled back into a short, sloppy ponytail, giving her a sexy 'here I am' look. Her dark–rimmed glasses no longer made her look nerdy to him, but rather sophisticated in a Ph.D. candidate sort of way.

He smiled as his gaze wandered from the hair tie she wore, past the T–shirt and tight–fitting jeans, down to her feet. She wore comfortable clothes, indeed clothes not meant to impress, and she appeared at peace with herself.

She looked radiant in a complete banana split kind of way. A natural beauty not needing the expensive outfits and caked on makeup. Someone who probably tumbled out of bed looking sexy.

Her voice sounded even–toned as she continued to read. Her pacing was smooth and deliberate. The only other sound he heard was a slight rumbling from her stomach. She paused in her task, placed her hand on her belly, and said, "Excuse me."

She cleared her throat and began reading again. Her voice sounded professional, but Daniel had difficulty concentrating. It was late, and he was also hungry.

And then he remembered the tweets that rumored that Deborah was pregnant. That would explain why she seemed more beautiful tonight than ever before. She was glowing.

A heaviness settled in the pit of his stomach as he watched her scroll down the page on her laptop and continued reading.

She sported a new look, probably for a fresh start with a new man. If he remembered correctly, she was about the same age as he was...maybe just a few years younger. When was her birthday? January? He must have just missed it.

His stomach rumbled, and he glanced at the time. Was it already after eight o'clock?

The refrigerator might be bare since he'd been gone a few days, but he needed to get something together for dinner. Deborah was probably starving since she was eating for two, although her pregnancy didn't show with the skinny jeans she wore.

Giving her a sideways glance, he studied her belly. He didn't see what the photographer had referred to as a baby bump. Of course, Deborah had always been lean and trim.

Professionally polished.

Respectful.

Sexy as hell.

She shifted on the couch and folder her legs under her.

Damn, they were skinny jeans.

Nice and tight.

He cleared his throat and focused. "I'm going to order something to eat. What would you like?" he asked the second she'd finished reading.

She picked up some paperwork next to her on the couch and sifted through a few pages. "We're almost done here. I can wait until I'm back at the hotel to eat."

Already? It wasn't *that* late.

Overall, there wasn't that much work to do, and it could have waited until tomorrow. But Deborah wouldn't be at the office. He did need her help, and he absolutely wanted to see her. Given some more time, he could come up with more stuff to keep them busy.

"Don't be silly," he said with a hint of urgency. "There's at least another hour of work ahead of us. I'll order whatever you want, Deborah." Her name rolled off his tongue and felt natural for him to say. It was hard to think of her now as Ms. Baxter.

Her beautiful green eyes lit up as she set the paper down and made eye contact with him, staring at him for a moment. "You haven't eaten a home–cooked meal in nearly a week, Daniel. I'll make you something."

Her face lit up at the suggestion, but he couldn't have her cook. She was a guest in his home. "Deborah, you don't need to make something for dinner."

The dogs, who had been asleep by Deborah's feet, whined when they heard the word dinner. One sat up and nudged her with his nose.

"I guess you two are hungry, as well." She patted the dogs and then placed her glasses on the table. "Your standard grocery delivery should have arrived yesterday."

"Seems like my home practically runs itself." He let out a half-hearted chuckle. "I don't even have to be home."

No. He just needed Deborah and the magic wand she used to make everything perfect in his life.

"It takes some work. Trust me. Coordinating deliveries, running household errands… it can be time consuming."

She didn't sound upset, more matter–of–fact. It made him wonder how much time she spent here without him. He assumed it was quite a bit of time, seeing how the dogs loved up on her.

She stood and walked to the corner of the kitchen where a large bag of dog food lay. "Your dog walker came, your pantry service came… if it weren't so cold out, even your gardener would have come."

She scooped dry kibble and placed it in the two bowls on the floor. The Shelties ran over for their dinner, but didn't begin eating until she patted each one on the head. "I even had the pantry service bring more food for you guys, too. Yes, I did. Good boy, good girl."

His killer guard dogs just wanted to eat and then kiss Deborah all over.

He understood the feeling.

She had watched the dogs over the years, and if he remembered correctly, she had even suggested their names. The sable girl with reddish fur was named Ginger, and her merle brother with black fur was named Oreo. Ginger Snap and Oreo Cookie. Corny, but cute.

Daniel walked around the kitchen island. The room looked clean and sterile. He wondered if his maid service had just come by, as well. For someone who didn't hire domestic help, and only trusted Deborah into his home, she certainly had a team of people that came and took care of the place—all seamlessly with him not around.

Deborah washed her hands and then grabbed an apron from a counter drawer. She began tying the strings behind her when he took several quick steps to close the gap between them. "Let me help."

Standing directly behind her, he smelled the scent of her shampoo. It wasn't a fruity smell, but a delicate floral one. He inhaled deeply as his fingers took the apron straps from her hand.

He tied the thin fabric belt around her tiny waist.

Leaning toward her and feeling caught in a spell, he whispered into her ear, "Too tight?"

"It's fine."

The two of them paused and stood for a moment together. Her body radiated warmth, and he leaned in. With her hair pulled back, he saw the shapely curve of her neck. He inhaled deeply and paused just short of kissing her.

The moment felt like déjà–vu.

He had lived this scene before.

His body stiffened and he stopped breathing.

Everything felt too familiar.

Way too familiar.

He stepped back, allowing her to continue with the meal.

Glancing around the kitchen, he saw nothing out of the ordinary. His dishes. His dogs. His pots and pans. Evidently his apron. His girlfriend... A smile came to his lips. No. Not his girlfriend. His Deborah.

A feeling of electricity shocked his body and he stared at the back of Deborah's head as she gathered cooking utensils.

His Deborah.

This kitchen, this scene... it had all been in a dream the other night with his brunette–haired mystery woman. The woman he had dreamt about every night while in California.

He felt a pain in the pit of his stomach, and his

mouth went dry. It couldn't be. He stared at Deborah's beautiful head of hair. *She* was his dream brunette.

God. It was her. His mystery dream woman was Deborah... His knees melted under him, and he nearly stumbled.

She wasn't even facing him, and yet he knew hers was the face he never got to see in his dreams.

He couldn't stop himself. His legs may have felt like Jell-O, but they moved him across the floor. For a moment, he leaned in. He smelled her intoxicating scent, heard the soft tune she hummed, and felt her body warmth so close to him.

What was he doing? This was Ms. Baxter... Deborah. It was Deborah. His assistant.

He raked his hand through his hair and stepped back, giving himself distance from her.

She walked to the refrigerator and inspected the fully stocked shelves, finally settling on salmon and fresh vegetables.

"Why don't you continue with the paperwork? This will take some time."

Her voice sounded strained as if she had noticed him standing too close to her, but she was the one who had moved away and denied him the kiss.

He watched as she elegantly made her way around the kitchen grabbing spices, mixing bowls, and knives. She knew his place better than he did. Hell, he hadn't even known he owned an apron until he'd seen her pull it out of the drawer.

"Go on. I'll call you when dinner is ready."

"If you wouldn't mind, I'd rather finish the paperwork with you." He didn't know what else to say. I need you? I've been dreaming of you? I have feelings for you?

He settled on, "Together we seem to get through the paperwork a lot faster."

"Of course, sir."

He was a coward. Sure, their romantic relationship was a fake. And she was probably seeing another man. And, he couldn't forget, she may be pregnant.

His chest tightened. There were a lot of reasons to be a coward. She probably didn't even feel the same way about him.

Feeling useless, he glanced around the room and found nothing to do. Noticing that he still wore the wrinkled suit from his flight, he said, "I'd like to shower and get the airport smell off me."

"Of course, sir."

24

A kiss.

Daniel had almost kissed her.

No reporters. No witnesses. She wasn't the heiress this time. She was Deborah.

Just Deborah in his kitchen making him a meal.

Her heart raced and she could feel her pulse in her throat.

She needed to distance herself from Daniel. Not with just a line in the sand but a freaking wall with barbed wire.

She paced; her breath staggered with nervous gulps of air.

Hell, no. She wasn't going to scale that wall. She was going to stick with the plan. Make dinner. Eat dinner. Leave. Keep Daniel at arm's length away from her heart.

Okay. She could do this.

Taking in a deep breath, she shook out her hands and rotated her head from side to side. Distance. That's all she needed.

She julienned the carrots while listening to the shower running upstairs. She should have stuck with her first plan and powered through the paperwork and then left. Why had she suggested making him dinner?

Well, she *was* hungry.

Plus, she'd enjoyed this evening. Work aside, she'd missed Daniel.

She glanced down at the hallway outside the kitchen where his suitcase stood. How many times had she unpacked for him and organized his dry cleaning?

Being a personal assistant had an aspect of the job right in the title. Personal. She knew what toothpaste he used, what medicines he took, and what type of underwear he wore.

Boxers.

Her head tilted toward the ceiling. He was wearing nothing now.

No. She took a deep breath and tried to focus on something else.

The engagement ring sparkled, and she looked at it. She felt a twinge of pain in her gut. Being a personal assistant didn't mean she needed to play the part of fictitious fiancée, be paraded around on dates, and kept in the best hotel in town. But, deep down, she enjoyed the role.

Ginger nudged her.

"Don't look at me like that," Deborah said. "I'm not doing anything wrong."

Two sets of warm brown puppy eyes stared at her expectantly.

"I'm not your mommy, so stop begging."

God, they looked adorable.

She tossed a small piece of carrot to both of the dogs, who gulped them down and looked up for more.

She took out the grill top and basket for the stove. All she needed to do now was make some rice. If she could find any.

Nearly tripping over the dogs, she made her way to the freezer and found a frozen bag of brown rice. Microwave fast and ready in only five minutes.

The sooner she left the better.

She glanced up. The shower still ran. Okay, she just needed to finish, eat, and bid a hasty retreat—all while keeping her clothes on.

Her hands shook when she heard the water stop, so she set the knife down and stopped chopping vegetables. He was out of the shower and naked.

No. She wasn't going to think about him toweling off the beads of water that rolled down his muscular chest and back. Didn't want to imagine his wet, bare footprints as they marked the tile floor in the bathroom. She especially didn't want to think about the rest of his body.

So why was she slowly making her way from the kitchen and up to his bedroom?

Daniel stepped out of the shower, his preheated towel draped around his waist. Water dripped down to the floor tile, but he didn't pay it any attention. Deborah was his dream woman. Deborah.

He checked his watch. Only ten minutes had passed. He didn't want to keep her waiting.

He stood in front of the foggy mirror wearing nothing but the towel. Staring at his reflection, he wondered if he should shave. If he did, he could wear aftershave.

His head felt as fogged up as the mirror. Using a hand towel, he cleared the glass and saw himself clearer. He even opened the bathroom door to let in some cool air. Unfortunately, he couldn't clear his mind as easily.

He had known her all these years and had never appreciated her until now.

But this wasn't a date. Deborah was only here to help him with the paperwork, and she needed to remain off–limits. Off–limits since Ellington–Weston employed her, and…she was probably with another man and having his baby—that was if the many postings on his phone app were accurate.

But could you trust everything you read on the Internet?

Daniel paced the bathroom floor.

Why did he have such a stupid policy of not dating employees?

Pregnant employees? Forget it. Those needed to be doubly off–limits.

But who was she dating? Someone from work? Hopefully, the man would treat her better than Josh's father, whoever he was. Daniel didn't want Deborah to become a single mother again. He knew she was capable, but she deserved more than that.

He brushed his teeth and combed through his hair, trying to distract himself from the idea that he may have missed his chance with her.

Another five minutes passed, and he needed to go downstairs. He could at least help her with the dinner or set the table.

He could do this. She was downstairs in the kitchen. They had eaten dinner plenty of times together in the past. Dinner. Work. Then she'd leave.

No problem.

He entered his bedroom and felt the cool breeze of the ceiling fan as the air hit his bare chest and helped dry off the water from the shower. Hearing footsteps behind him, he turned to find Deborah entering his room.

She walked through the opened door. "I bought

you more shampoo and conditioner," she said, staring at the towel. "I also bought new household linens."

Problem.

He didn't bring his dates to his home—his private oasis, his haven. No one penetrated his security barrier. No one except Deborah.

She was here, now, in his room.

She looked gorgeous.

"I missed your birthday last month." His voice was soft with a hint of an apology in it. It was all he could think of to say to her.

"It was last week."

He stepped closer to her, his body pulled toward her, and his feet merely obeying. "I'm sorry I forgot."

Deborah obviously had been in his bedroom before, most likely hanging up dry cleaning or packing him for a trip. It had never occurred to him that she would be so familiar with him in such a personal way. The only difference was that he had never stood bare in front of her before with just a towel between the two of them.

Her hair hung free from her pony tail and cascaded down her cheeks in a sexy, tumbled way. Her skin invited him, begging for his touch. Licking his lips, he stared at hers. They were red and plump. They needed to be devoured.

Her gaze drifted down and on the towel. He watched as her eyes lingered for several seconds, causing him to grip the knot tightly.

She licked her lips and he heard a slight sigh, her gaze still plastered on the green terrycloth—which was quickly tenting in the front.

His heart raced and threatened to explode. The private room, the taboo status, and the world disappeared—leaving just a man and a woman.

He darted across the room, removing his hand from the towel and engulfing her in his arms.

He lifted her off the ground and her legs circled around his waist. His hands wrapped around her back and sought out her firm bottom.

He held her closer to him and the thin towel, which had loosened with his steps and began to slide down his hips.

She let out a soft gasp and he claimed her lips with his. Drops of water from his chest moistened her shirt, which now clung to her. The sweet smell of lilacs from her shampoo became stronger as the ringlets touched his cheeks.

She molded her legs tighter around his hips. He cupped his hands around her firm cheeks to hold her better. His manhood pushed against the plush towel, finally undoing the twisted knot from his waist allowing his massive rod to stroke against her.

He moved them closer to the bed, noticing that her hand had gripped the towel and tugged it away, causing them both to tumble. The screeching of the springs increased as they hit the mattress.

The dampness of her white T–shirt allowed him to

see a lacy red bra. He lifted the damp shirt, caressed her silky–smooth skin, and kissed her chest.

Her perfectly round breasts pressed against him, nearly spilling from the lacy cups. He pulled one side down, allowing the nipple to peek above the garment. He licked the pebbled flesh, eliciting a loud moan from her.

Was she a screamer? He nibbled at her breast, wanting to find out.

He pulled the T–shirt off and then unclasped the bra. She arched her back as his hand kneaded one exposed mound of flesh.

Her jeans needed to come off, and right now. He halfway sat up so he could remove them, and Deborah took the opportunity to tightly grasp his throbbing member. She stroked him hard.

Up and down.

Her touch wasn't making this task any easier.

"One sec," he managed to say as he stood.

Now standing next to the bed, he yanked her pants off and revealed the matching red lace underwear beneath. Nice, but entirely in the way. He ripped them from her body and found her dark brunette curls. Her passionate scent filled the air, and he inhaled deeply, knowing that she was dripping wet for him.

Her legs spread wide, inviting him in, as she moaned his name.

He reached into the nightstand for a condom and ripped open the shiny, foil package. His fingertips fumbled with the item, rolling the thick circle's edge until he could easily put it on.

She took it from his hands and placed it on him, her hand stroking his swollen manhood as she unrolled it to the hilt of his length. "You were taking too long."

Just by the look she gave him, her breathy voice, and the way she had touched him—especially with the scent of her sweet arousal filling the air—the evening could have ended before it began.

He needed to be inside her. Now.

Lying on top of her firm and beautiful body, he plunged himself deeply within her slickened folds where she was dripping with desire.

Deborah's eyes closed, and she let out a gasp. "Oh, God." Her hands gripped his bottom, and her knees lifted up, setting him deeper. She repeatedly said, "Yes," as she dug her fingernails into his flesh.

She felt tight, really tight, and damn good. He pulled out his length and plunged into her again and again, curving his body and holding her tightly as if he needed to meld with her and become one person.

She thrust her hips to match his rhythm, causing the bedsprings to squeak even more.

He kissed her slender neck, and his cheek brushed against hers. She was moaning and breathing heavily, which egged him on.

The pace sped up. Damn. His balls tightened, and he knew he was about to come. He plunged into her hard several more times before his head flung back and his body went taut. He released into the condom just as her body spasmed. He felt her tightening around his length, milking him.

His breathing became labored and his heart raced. She was a vision with her hair splayed across the pillow and the satisfied look on her face.

Eighteen years he had known her. He gently massaged her shoulder and grinned at her. "We should have been doing this the entire time."

25

A jostling on the bed stirred Deborah, nearly waking her. A shift, a movement, and then a wet tongue licking her face caused her to jerk her hand toward the disruption.

"Woof."

Oreo lay on the bed softly kissing her. She smiled at the dog and tried to go back to sleep. A whine on the floor gave away Ginger's location.

A jolt of reality—the type you get when a world crashes down on you—ran through her now stiffened body.

No, No, No

She gazed over to where she heard soft snoring and found Daniel peacefully sleeping. The blanket bunched near his left thigh and she could see his firm butt cheek peeking out.

A quick peek under the covers and she found herself naked as well.

Oh, God.

A pain twisted in her gut.

Her boss.

She had slept with her boss.

It wasn't a dream.

Stupid. Stupid. Stupid.

Her father's harsh words—you need self-respect, take pride in your work, be valued for your skills—pounded in her mind, ricocheting off mental walls and echoing in her brain.

What she needed was an escape plan, but all she wanted to do was to shrivel up and disappear—hard to do with a dog licking your face, its tail swishing from side-to-side and threatening to wake Daniel at any moment.

"Shhhh," she said to the dogs.

She lay still and petted Oreo while she thought of what to do next.

Leave and pretend nothing happened? Stay and have some breakfast?

Shrivel up and become a nun?

Whether she wanted to admit it or not, the night had been special. It had been sensual. It had also been stupid.

But she was the one who entered the bedroom. She had made the decision.

Her muscles ached, but in a good way. Sex was

like riding a bike. It might have been years since she'd been with a man, but it all came back.

Hell, it was like she had won the freakin' French Open. They had made love not once, but three times.

Initially, she'd thought she paled in comparison to his vast experience. But maybe that was what had made the night even more magical. He'd acted like a man dying of thirst with her holding the only bottle of water in town.

And that little trick he did with his tongue... Whoever had taught him that was a genius.

Wetness pooled within her core as she studied his firm body. All those gym renewals she had done for him over the years had certainly paid off. She was never one to slack off with physical fitness either, but thank God she'd decided to work out at the hotel gym the last four days.

Shit. She needed to stop staring at his bare ass peeking out from the covers.

Daniel was off limits.

She tried to envision his body covered with rashes and flab, but her memory of his lean form kept popping into her mind.

She closed her eyes and took in a deep breath. The sun had risen, which meant the night, and, if she knew anything about Daniel, the one–night stand, were over. At best, she might get a few good months of being with him, but at what cost? Once Daniel grew bored with her, he'd toss her aside—and then she'd lose her job and the money Josh needed for college.

Josh! What had she done? She was such an idiot.

She felt as though punched in the gut. A dozen scenarios played in her mind in an instant, and none of them had a happily ever after.

Once Daniel tossed her aside, the scholarship money would be gone, as well.

She inched one foot from under the covers and searched for the floor. Shifting her bare bottom, she scooted herself away from Daniel to leave the bed. His hand loosened, and she could slide her arm out from under his.

Shifting out from the covers to a kneeling position on the floor, she kept an eye on him and listened to his breathing.

So far, so good.

She had to leave here with some shred of dignity, and hope that the two of them could remain professional at work, at least until Josh graduated.

The light from the window cast a warm glow across her naked body as she tiptoed to a pile of clothing on the floor that she recognized as hers.

She picked up each item. Jeans. T–shirt. One shoe. She made her way to the center of the room where more clothes lay. *Another shoe. Bra...* Where were her panties?

"If you're looking for your underwear, I tossed them on the chair last night once I ripped them off you." Daniel leaned up in bed with one arm stretched out to her. "Where are you going?" He lay open to her not bothering to cover up.

Using her clothes to hide as best she could and avoiding eye contact with him or his throbbing member, she walked to the chair and her torn panties.

"You have a meeting early this morning. A merger meeting." It was the only thing she could think of, and she had no idea what time it was since he had only mentioned it to her last night, but talking about work seemed like the safest topic at the moment.

He picked up his watch from the nightstand and checked the time. "There's no rush. Scott will understand if I was a few minutes late."

Her fingers traced the lace panties, noting the rip.

Why did she have to wear red, sexy underwear? She was a mother, his employee, a church goer….

He patted the mattress and gave her a puppy-dog face that neither Ginger nor Oreo could pull off.

The tug of the look almost proved too much, and she nearly caved, but gathered her resolve instead.

"And my father will just be happy to be at the office meeting with old friends until we get there," he said.

The panties were a lost cause, but she managed to put her bra on at lightning speed. "What? … Your father will be in the office today?"

Daniel slowly sat up, disappointment showing in

his face as the dogs jumped on the bed to greet him. "Let's not talk about my father."

"He's in Chicago?"

"He may be retired, but he's still interested in the business." Daniel patted both Oreo and Ginger, both wanting attention. "He wasn't at the conference and wants to get caught up with what's going on."

"The merger. Of course." That's all it was. Regular business stuff. She pulled her T–shirt over her head and put on her jeans. Her socks were missing in action so she tossed on her sneakers without them.

She took in a deep breath. Of course, he'd be here on business.

"I suspect he's heard the rumor that I'm engaged and expecting a baby. I need to straighten him out."

Her knees felt like rubber and she staggered to the chair to sit. Vincent Ellington was at the office and was under the impression that she was pregnant.

A pregnant Deborah to help and protect. An employee who made a regrettable decision. A single mom who could barely make ends meet.

She hadn't seen her old boss since he'd retired years ago, and this scenario felt a bit too familiar.

"He thinks that I…" Deborah pointed to herself as she stood and began pacing. "That I… God, I can't see him. Not like this. Not after everything he did for me."

"*Everything* he did for you?"

She felt sick to her stomach, and her hand covered her mouth. "I think I'm going to throw up."

Daniel grabbed his robe from the side of the bed and put it on. He then gestured to the ensuite bathroom. "Morning sickness?"

Deborah's stomach now flip-flopped and she gawked at him. "Wait. Now *you* think I'm pregnant?"

She stared at him, knowing now how it feels to have your legs tossed out from under you. "How can I be pregnant?"

"What?"

"Oh, puh-lease." Her hands tensed and her tone became sarcastic. "I can only pretend so much."

His eyes lit up, and he stared at her belly. "You're *not* pregnant?"

"God, no." Her body went taut with anger. Daniel had been in on this farce since the beginning. He was her partner in this crime. "Why do you think I'm pregnant?" She gazed down at her stomach. "Do I *look* pregnant?"

"A few websites reported that you were."

"Fake. It's all been a lie between us."

She stood and glared at him and waved her hands in the air mockingly. "I'm the wealthy, now-pregnant Austrian heiress that you're pretending to marry."

She took deep breaths and felt the room close in on her, making it hard to breath. "All these years…" A prickling headache was forming. "I've learned nothing."

She stared at him. "I've learned *nothing*. I…I don't even have alcohol to blame this time."

"What are you talking about?"

"I slept with my boss… again."

"Again?" Daniel shook his head and tried to put his arm around her, only to have her shrug him off.

"Deborah, you're making no sense. Last night was…"

"A mistake." Her gaze darted to him, and her stomach twisted. "The last time it was all a lie. A lie just to get me into bed. Now, it's another lie. A lie to… to what? To fool the world? To get you off some list?"

He gestured to the chair. "Perhaps you should sit down."

"History is repeating itself. And I jumped right in and played my part." She tugged off the ring and tossed it on a nearby table. "Not anymore. I quit."

26

*D*eborah had to escape.

The lie she was living, the broken promise to herself, and betraying of Josh and his financial future were just too much.

She ran down the stairs, grabbed her purse from the couch, and ran out of the house—triggering the outside alarm. Daniel yelled and chased after her, but she couldn't even face him.

Between the alarm, his yelling, and the dogs barking, she could hardly think.

Keys.

Need keys.

She fumbled through her purse, found her keys, and quickly got into the car. Without even buckling her seat belt, she raced to the outside gate only to pause once she got there.

Her phone was in her purse. One click of the safety app, and doing her seat belt, the gate opened and she raced to the highway.

Tears streamed down her cheeks, and before she realized it, she was headed to Sue's house. She needed some sister time.

The two dogs went on massive bark patrol and nearly tripped Daniel as he tried to catch Deborah.

He watched as she drove down the path to the estate's gate, leaving him and all of his questions unanswered.

Her words lingered in his thoughts. Had she quit being his wife or his assistant? Or had she quit being both?

"Quiet. Oreo. Ginger," he yelled, his hands and voice enunciating each word.

He ran to the control panel in the kitchen and shut off the alarm, typing in the secret 'all clear signal' so the police would not come.

He sat on a stool, surrounded by the dirty dishes from their late-night snack—the dinner stored in the fridge for another time.

What the hell had just happened?

The dogs stood by the door whining, so he let them out and set out their breakfast.

All these years he thought he understood Deborah. After spending one night with her, she'd turned into someone he couldn't read at all.

He heard his alarm upstairs and knew he probably should care that it was time for him to get up and start the day. The alarm, the merger, the workday… he didn't care. He needed to talk with Deborah. Find out what went so terribly wrong and whatever it took, he had to fix it.

Once upstairs, he called her several times, but she didn't answer.

One question plagued him. She'd said she had slept with her boss *again*, but they'd only been together last night. Thinking back to how *complete* she had made him feel, he wasn't willing to accept that their lovemaking was a mistake.

And yet, she'd said she had made the same mistake as before.

Mistake.

He needed to see her.

Figuring she'd be at the hotel or her house, Daniel showered and got ready. One cold fact dominated his thoughts. Deborah had worked as his father's secretary before becoming his.

He couldn't breath.

He thought of the timeline and of Josh's age, and began to feel light headed.

Had Deborah been his father's mistress?

Daniel needed at least one antacid, probably more.

He couldn't find Deborah and she wasn't answering her phone. Not wanting to go home, he decided to go into work. Perhaps the work day would help get his mind off of the shit of the morning.

The crowd that had formed in the lobby of his office building fueled his anger. The damn list is what started the whole mess, and he didn't need to see the press today.

The crowd had swarmed the lobby of the office complex, but he ignored his claustrophobia and parted the crowd like the Red Sea.

Brandelynn separated from the shadows as he rounded the security desk. "Daniel, we need to talk."

His heart skipped a beat, but not in a good way. The police had told him not to interact with her, and his inner voice screamed for him to run, but he held his ground. Her voice sounded commanding, and he didn't like her tone. "We have nothing to say to each other."

An evil smirk crossed her face as though she had the upper hand. "Then I'll talk with Didi, or should I say, *Ms. Baxter*."

Hearing Brandelynn say Deborah's name caused him to pause. Deborah hadn't been answering her phone, and he didn't know where she was right now. Could Brandelynn have somehow hurt her?

He walked her to the corner of the security desk as far away from the reporters as he could, but not before catching the eye of the guard at the desk. Brandelynn may be wearing a hat and sunglasses, but this had been the same employee that had let her into the building over the last few months—and he had been warned to keep an eye out for her. He got the hint; Daniel noticed a nod from the man and then him quickly reaching for the phone.

"Just say what you want to say and then leave," he said, his voice low as he hid any hint of concern over Deborah's safety—not wanting to give Brandelynn the upper hand.

She glared at him with crazed eyes, and his body stiffened. That stare, where someone viewed you as only a meal ticket seared into him all the way down to his bones. It was the look from his past, the one from his nightmares as a child.

He took a deep breath and stood straighter. He wasn't a small kid anymore, separated from his mother. He was in control. 'Crazy eyes' would not deter him today, nor would he allow her to hurt Deborah.

Her hands gestured in the air as though she were taking in a giant billboard. "Billionaire uses personal assistant to get off the Top 10 Bachelor list." She took a deep breath and shook her head. "I'm still working on the title."

"Find an editor," he said in a snide tone. The

anxiety bubbled within his gut, and he needed her to come out and say what she had come here to say.

"Whatever I come up with, the title needs to be something to get you and Ms. Battle-Axe back," she paused, "I mean, you and Ms. Baxter back for what you've done."

"What *we've* done?" He knew Brandelynn's con was against him, but he didn't realize there'd be a vendetta against Deborah for her foiling Brandelynn's plans. He never should have brought Deborah into his lie.

"What you've done?" She rolled her eyes. "I followed you the last few days. Camped out, and froze my butt off at the Langtham Hotel just for a glimpse of your betrothed. I was quite surprised to see Ms. Baxter as your Australian heiress." She glanced around the room. "She's late getting here this morning."

Daniel was able to breath once again. Brandelynn didn't know where Deborah was, and obviously her brother didn't either. He needed her to stay here until the police arrived.

"My lie couldn't have been that bad if you've been following the two of us around for days." He didn't wait for her to comment. "I understand your brother works for a magazine. I know he's your partner."

Her eyes gave away the secret, even if she didn't comment on the remark.

"Your bother followed me that day I went shopping and recorded me. He's the one who uploaded that baby store video to the Internet."

"That's a wonderful little story, but I don't know what you're talking about. I'm an only child," her voice was condescending, and full of lies.

She glared at him as if trying to brainwash him with laser vision. "A security zealot like you won't want this headline spread all over the news. All I'm asking for is a few thousand dollars to keep my mouth shut."

Her words sounded shaky. He suspected her brother usually did the arm twisting with her... well, with her fucking her way to fortune.

From the corner of his eye, Daniel could see two detectives in regular clothing talking with the guard. They would hopefully follow her and arrest both her and her brother.

Daniel leaned in—ignoring her insane expression —and closed the distance between them so he'd be menacing right in her face. "How about this? I give you and your brother exactly one hour to run before I report your whereabouts to the police in Nebraska." Each word was said as though they were backed with a sledgehammer. "I'm sure they'll want to talk to you. Hell, there may even be a reward for tipping them off."

Her face reddened, and he knew he had bested her.

He gestured to catch the attention of the security guard. "I don't ever want to see you or your brother again."

"Yes, sir?" the guard said.

"This woman needs to be escorted from the building. See to it that she doesn't return."

He left Brandelynn where she stood and walked to the elevator, the guard's 'yes sir' trailing off into the background. The guard would escort her out and Brandelynn would believe he was done with her. Then, the detectives would follow her. She was now their problem.

Even if she didn't lead them to her brother, Daniel suspected that she'd talk and rat out him out, or that she'd do the jail time again and let him get off scott free. Either way, they were out of his life for good.

A sense of accomplishment engulfed him, and he felt proud to have defeated the con artists, but the feeling was fleeting. He still didn't know where Deborah was.

Continuing on to his office, he noticed two women standing next to the elevator and pointing at an announcement on the bulletin board. As he walked past, he glanced at the paper. Seeing his picture had him stopping mid–step and backing up.

The women whispered and made room for him when he got closer. His breath hitched when he saw his name in bold print and highlighted. He was the number one bachelor in all of Chicago. He scanned the article and noticed a coppery taste as he clenched his jaw and bit his lower lip.

His life was all about providing security to companies, and he felt the heat of his cheeks as he saw that not only his full name, age, and occupation were listed in the article, so was his home address and salary.

You've got to be kidding me.

"Cute and rich," one of the women whispered.

"Hush. You're already married," whispered the other one.

Daniel ripped the sheet off the board and crumpled it, balling it into his fist. He had always felt safe in his own company, but now there was a target on his back, an opening for every crazed woman out there to attack him. The elevator doors opened, so he got in and hit the top floor's button.

He understood that his personal information was within the public domain of the Internet. People just had to look it up. But to have it plastered like wallpaper in his office building? It was too much.

He told himself that the publicity was only a nuisance to start his day, one that he didn't have time for. All he wanted to do was spend the day with Deborah, and now he was caught up in all of this shit.

He exited on his floor and tossed the crumpled piece of paper into the closest trash can.

Entering his office, he discovered the lights off. They were never off. It meant that he was the first to arrive.

Goddamit.

He took a deep breath and slowly cursed at how dreadful this day had already become.

He turned on the lights and scanned the room, taking note of how lonely the room felt. No coffee had been made, no warm greeting waited, no mail was stacked on his desk... The room felt cold and uninviting. His assistant, Ms. Ortiz, must be running late. Either that or she was goofing off.

Judging by the paperwork piled up on her desk, he figured the reason was probably both.

He leafed through the paperwork thrown haphazardly on his desk, placing it into two neat piles —one to look through later and one marked "Urgent."

God, some of this stuff he should have taken care of before he'd left for the conference.

He walked around the desk and gathered more of the mail, his foot brushing up against papers that had fallen to the floor.

In the mix lay next year's scholarship paperwork for Josh.

Another heavy weight fell upon his shoulders and he felt his muscles tighten. Daniel hadn't signed the renewal yet, and it needed to go out right away.

Staring at the envelope, he thought of the young man. His dark hair, green eyes, and height should have been a dead giveaway that the boy was an Ellington. Not just any Ellington either, the boy was his half-brother.

Shit.

He tasted bitterness in his throat. His father had touched Deborah. He had... been with her. Felt the softness of her skin, the deliciousness of her lips, and the dampness of her folds.

Worse yet, the damn married man had thrown Deborah aside with a baby, all while stabbing his mother in the back.

Daniel would never have wanted his mother to be hurt by such an affair. How could his father have been so cruel to both of them?

Josh hadn't grown up privileged. He'd lived paycheck–to–paycheck and had a mother who sacrificed everything for him. He was a good kid and deserved better. How could his father deny the boy all these years?

The fact that Daniel had slept with his half-brother's mother played heavily on his mind. Some amount of incest existed in that reality, one that Daniel didn't want to think about since he... He swallowed the lump in his throat and a pain deep in his gut boomed. He loved Deborah.

Touching the back of her empty chair, his fingers felt the smoothness of the leather. This was her spot in his life, and he had only now really seen her.

All this time, she had kept a huge secret from him.

He should be upset, but all he could think about was how she must have sacrificed time and money to raise the boy on her own.

Shaking his head, he entered his office and tossed the scholarship paperwork on his desk. He then turned on the lights. The window shades remained drawn, so he gave a halfhearted attempt to search for the remote to open them. He couldn't find the damn thing.

Checking the clock on the far wall, he was fifteen minutes late to his meeting, and yet Scott was nowhere to be found either. Of course, no assistant sat in the outer office to welcome him, give him a cup of coffee, and ask him to take a seat while he waited.

Hearing footsteps in the hallway, he walked back into the assistant area and peeked out the open door to see Ms. Ortiz marching toward him. She held a Starbucks cup in one hand and her phone in the other.

She entered the office and stared at him. Her eyes grew wide, and a smile spread across her lips as she put her phone away. Her expression wasn't one of shame at being caught arriving late to the job, and she didn't apologize either. Oh, no. The look she gave him differed from her usual 'my boss is handsome.' Today's look was more of a 'my boss is worth billions, and I must have him.'

She knew about the list.

Fuck. *Everybody* knew about the damn list.

Did all women monitor the Top 10 list searching

for their prey? Didn't they have more pressing issues like their careers or education or family to attend to?

She set her coffee down and then swung her purse off her shoulder. It landed on one stack of paper on her desk with a thud, scattering the pile. When she took off her coat, she wasn't shy about parading her cleavage in front of him.

He felt like a small animal caught in a cave with a tigress. But this cave belonged to him, and he wasn't about to be hunted on his own territory.

"You're late," Daniel said in a voice that shook the room. He removed his coat and walked into his office. Placing the garment on the rack and his work satchel on his desk, he turned and looked at her. "I have a meeting…now with the company lawyer. I don't see him, so he may be in the guest office."

"Looks like his office light is finally on," came a familiar voice from the hallway.

After knowing the man for years, he recognized Scott's booming voice from a mile away. He'd come to discuss the legal issues within the new merger; the merger Deborah had helped him with last night before joining him in his bedroom.

They never did get a chance to finish the document or dinner or any other merger details. His lips curled into a smile as he remembered some of the details of why.

Another voice came from the hallway. It too sounded familiar. It was the one man Daniel wasn't ready to confront just yet, and he wasn't pleased when his father moved his wheelchair into the office.

"Son! It's good to see you." Vincent Ellington opened his arms wide to hug him, but Daniel forced himself to give just a cold, half-hearted side-hug.

"Scott was just filling me in on a few things."

Daniel stared at his father. Deborah had worked for him for a brief period before rejoining the secretarial pool, making her available to become Daniel's assistant. With his mother now deceased, he wondered if his father's marriage had been as happy as Daniel always assumed it to be. Perhaps there was more going on than he'd ever noticed.

God, what if Deborah wasn't the only woman.

Ms. Ortiz hovered around her desk—Deborah's desk—and looked out of place like a cat showing up at a premier dog show. She stared at Vincent Ellington, which made Daniel wonder if the Top 10 Bachelor complete article about him had mentioned that his father was also wealthy.

Ms. Ortiz eyed Vincent as though she didn't mind winning silver, especially with an older man. Daniel couldn't let his lecherous father to be a victim of a shallow bitch like her.

Daniel picked up the phone and pressed the red button. "Ms. Ortiz was just leaving. Escort her from the building." He turned to face her and, in his most commanding Donald Trump voice, he said, "You're fired."

"What?" Ms. Ortiz spilled her coffee walking over to him. "I was just a few minutes late."

As she rattled off why he was too hasty, he opened the door to his office and told Scott and his father to make themselves comfortable. Daniel waited just long enough for security to come and collect the temp before joining the men in his office.

"Your new assistant was terrible," Scott said.

"Tell me something I don't know," Daniel said.

"What's going on with Deborah?" Scott moved a chair out of the way so Vincent could slide in closer to the desk.

"I filled your father in on the ruse while we were waiting for you, especially since he saw a posted article in the lobby about you making that dreaded list."

Daniel stared at his father and his jaw tightened. The man had said he wanted to talk about Deborah. He took the merger document out from his work satchel and gripped it firmly.

"Deborah is doing well." He took a seat at his desk and rubbed his fingers across the paperwork. In his coldest tone he could muster, he said, "The contract has ended, as well as her employment."

"What?" Vincent asked. "Please tell me you didn't fire her because she couldn't keep you off that list."

"I didn't fire her. She quit."

Had the announcement that she was leaving upset

his father? Whatever they might have had between them had ended a long time ago.

"Did she say why she quit?" Scott asked.

Scott's voice held concern. He may be one of his best friends, but this was an employee matter. He wasn't about to discuss Deborah's decision in front of Scott, at least not until her employee dissolution paperwork from the company was drafted. He felt a pain in the pit of his stomach at the thought of her no longer working for the company.

Working for him.

"She is leaving for personal reasons," he managed to choke out.

"Is she upset?" Scott asked.

Both men had a concerned expression on their faces, their worry for Deborah evident.

Daniel picked up a pen from his desk and fiddled with it, trying to recapture a business atmosphere. "She might be upset."

"She can't sue the company, right?" Vincent glared at Scott.

"No, sir. The contract's fine print made sure of that."

Daniel's gaze ping–ponged between the two, and he felt as if they shared a secret. He hated secrets. "What are you two talking about?"

A blank stare crossed Vincent's face. It was a look Daniel had never seen on the man before. "Deborah, although she's never been a problem for this company and certainly an asset to you, has been a ticking time bomb just ready to explode."

"I found an opportunity to defuse the bomb, and I took it," Scott said. "She won't be an issue for this company."

27

a time bomb?

Daniel understood how shrewd the lawyer could be, which was why Daniel kept Scott on the Ellington–Weston payroll.

If Deborah were a ticking time bomb, it meant that Scott knew about the affair. His friend knew and hadn't mentioned a word to him.

Damn secrets!

"What *fine print*?" Daniel's fingers gripped the pen tightly, causing his knuckles to turn white.

Hearing Daniel's rage-filled voice caused Scott to sit straighter in his office chair. "The fake engagement contract made it quite clear that she could not hold this company liable for anything past or present in regards to any sexual harassment or consequences thereof," Scott explained.

Daniel caught Scott's gaze and he read between the lines. "Deborah's son is a rather big life changing consequence. You don't have to be so cavalier about protecting this company and screwing her over."

Silence filled the room to the point of it being deafening.

"Deborah told me everything about the affair." Daniel glared at his father.

Scott put on his best professional face and straightened his tie. "I'm here to do a job," he said in a matter–of–fact tone. "The gist is that she can't sue the company because of what happened in the past. She signed her rights away."

When Daniel glared at him, Scott added, "I even circled that section of the agreement and pointed it out to her before she signed it. Remember?"

Daniel narrowed his eyes at Scott, wishing he could read the man's mind. No wonder people hated lawyers so much. And why large corporations paid for the best to protect them. He wanted to lash out, but Scott wasn't the problem.

No. The problem would be his lecherous father.

No longer able to look at his father, Daniel stared at the closed window. Had his mother learned of the affair? If so, the betrayal must have cut her deeply. Perhaps she'd died never knowing. Would that be better or worse?

Furrowing his brow, Daniel felt the loss of his

mother and the loss of something else. Deborah's son, Josh, was his half–brother, one that he'd never gotten an opportunity to know outside of the boy's internships with the company.

"Deborah is a ticking time bomb because of your affair with her, which resulted in her son." His heart raced. He didn't want to accuse his father of anything, but couldn't help but to name, label, and showcase the elephant in the room.

Vincent's eyes widened, and his mouth fell agape. "I didn't… I never…."

Staring at his father, Daniel wondered how long the affair had lasted. Had he proudly boasted about sorted details and ruined her reputation?

"She was your secretary, someone whom you worked closely with before you threw her back into the secretarial pool, pregnant and alone." Daniel's face twisted with disgust. "You were an authority figure twice her age, and you used her."

Best friend or not, this wasn't something Daniel would normally have shared with Scott. But Scott remained under oath to remain discreet about company issues, plus, he apparently knew everything about the sorted affair already. He probably knew more details than Daniel.

"This is why I wanted to visit with you in person. To explain everything." Vincent's face grew red. "I *helped* Deborah. I made sure she had a job and every opportunity to find another one if she decided to leave the company. Besides, even if I had slept with her—which I didn't—how is that different from your revolving bedroom door and the younger women you carry on with?"

Daniel slammed his hand on the desk and glared at his father. "I've never slept with an employee who relied on me for her paycheck." His jaw tightened. "You treated Deborah like a prostitute the minute you took advantage of her."

Daniel wanted to scream, he wanted to beat his fist on the desk, he wanted to lash out and make his father pay.

For a man wheelchair-bound, Vincent pounded his hand against the armrest and, for a moment, resembled the I'm-the-boss-of-you-all force of his youth that needed to be reckoned with. "I most certainly did not."

Scott raised his hand to calm Vincent. "Daniel, the affair wasn't between Deborah and your father. It was between her and Carl Weston, your uncle."

Daniel's gaze darted to Scott and then back to his father.

He felt the muscles of his chest relax and he was able to breathe again.

Carl was his mother's brother and the co–founder of the company. He was an older man with a roving eye, and the rumors existed of him being quite the hound back in his day.

"You thought Deborah had an affair with *me*?"

Daniel heard the disdain in his father's voice.

Vincent shook his head and reseated himself firmly in the wheelchair. "I loved your mother and was always faithful to her."

The expression on his father's face looked sincere and very hurt that his son would make such an accusation.

"How the hell do you know this, and I don't?" Daniel asked Scott.

Scott adjusted his tie and shifted in his seat. "When I assumed legal responsibility for the company five years ago, your father told me the entire story before he retired. Deborah had a one–night stand with your uncle, which resulted in their child, Josh. There was no relationship between the two, and she never asked for any monetary compensation."

Daniel stared at his father, whose expression had softened with the truth now out.

Carl was *more* than twice her age. Deborah had been just a kid at the time.

God, that was disgusting.

Daniel thought of his uncle laying his hands on Deborah and nearly threw up. At least it hadn't been his father who had slept with her. No, it was his mother's older brother, who used women like Kleenex.

"Carl took advantage of her." Vincent pointed his finger at Scott and then back at Daniel. "That man slept with so many of our employees, he needed to be on a leash. We only knew about the baby because your mother and Deborah's mother were friends."

Daniel's gaze shifted to his father. "Mom knew Deborah's family?"

Vincent waved his hand dismissively. "Your mother was friends with everyone. Of course, not with the Baxter family after this mess came about. Your mother insisted we allow Deborah to find a place within our company if she chose to do so. She was given excellent compensation and bonuses, but we had hoped she would just leave. But then you chose her to be your assistant."

Daniel sat straighter in the chair and leaned in toward them. "I chose her because... Because *you* told me to pick an assistant that I wouldn't be tempted by." Daniel took a deep breath. "You said the best assistants were the ones with proven skills who wouldn't be a temptation. Legally speaking, you told me that you never wanted to invite a lawsuit or have a distraction like a romance to stand in my way, or in the way of this company becoming something great."

"I didn't think you'd pick her." Vincent shook his head and gave the slightest bit of an eye roll, one that said he still didn't believe his selection. "Of all the employees to choose from... And I couldn't tell you *not* to pick her. I thought you'd select one of the older, more seasoned women. Or, even one of the men."

Vincent shrugged and gave a wry smile. "Not that many male assistants existed all those years ago."

Scott lifted his hand and stopped the heated conversation. "Daniel, you're clearly attracted to Deborah, so why did you choose her be your assistant all those years ago?"

"I'm not *clearly* attracted to her." Finding it hard to make eye contact, he focused on the items on his desk as though he were taking inventory. The recently discovered scholarship paperwork—that still needed signing—gaining most of his concentration.

"I've never..." Daniel started. "Well, I wouldn't have... She's a beautiful woman, don't get me wrong, but..."

"She's a beautiful woman you've fantasized about for months in your dreams." Scott gently touched Vincent's arm. "Like I told you on the phone last week. Your son is in love with Deborah."

"I'm not in love with..." He had been dreaming of Deborah for months, he just didn't realize it.

"Bullshit." Scott shook his head. "You should admit that you have feelings for her."

Looking accusingly at his father, Daniel slumped back in his chair. "I initially picked Deborah to be my assistant because you said she was the best secretary you ever had."

"She was until Carl stole her away from me to attend a conference with him." Vincent eyed his son. "Back in the day, the company wasn't so well off. We couldn't afford for both of us to go to the meeting, so he went and took Deborah with him."

A grimace crossed Vincent's face. "He hand–selected her for the overnight business trip. I don't know the details, just that she… Well, they were never a couple. She felt horrible for the one–night stand, but still reported the incident to human resources. That's how I came to know about the tryst." He took a deep breath and let it out slowly, changing his voice to be more mellow. "She is a good Catholic girl, who made a mistake. She confided in me that she was never much of a drinker and had gotten drunk that night. She woke up the next morning not remembering a thing."

Daniel's heart went out to Deborah. She was innocent and sweet, and just a kid at the time. He thought back to how she'd refused to drink with him during their dates. She didn't want to make the same mistake with him as she had with his uncle.

But last night there'd been no alcohol. She'd willingly come into his bedroom and was the one to initiate their lovemaking. He hadn't taken advantage of her.

After a short silence, Scott said, "Even with the smaller company size back then, there must have been plenty of competent employees to choose from to be your assistant. Why pick Deborah if there wasn't something between you?"

Daniel's jaw tightened as he remembered the real

reason he had chosen her. "She was a pregnant woman who I assumed was happily married. A perfect fit for an assistant because I figured she wouldn't distract me."

"And now, after all this time, you have feelings for her?" Vincent asked.

Daniel's raked his fingers through his hair and stared at the still closed drapes. Why couldn't they leave him alone?

"Deborah's in love with Daniel, too," Scott said to Vincent. "Your son just doesn't realize it yet."

Did Scott know about what had happened between them last night? Deborah wouldn't have said a word to anyone, except maybe Scott's wife.

Damn it.

He had forgotten about that little feedback loop. "Did Deborah say something to Caroline?"

"She didn't need to." Scott stood and buttoned his jacket. "I'll be right back. I want to get something from my briefcase in my guest office."

After Scott had left the room, Vincent leaned in closer to his son. "Your mother started the company's scholarship as a way of ensuring that her nephew would be able to attend college. She would have been thrilled that you gave the money this year to Josh."

Daniel gazed down at the scholarship paperwork. "I didn't give it to him. He earned it." God, he needed to fill the documents out. After spending a week hidden, he was lucky to have found it at all.

Deborah would have ensured that he saw the paperwork, placing it on top of his daily mail instead of letting it slip off the secretary desk and to the floor. He let out a deep sigh. He missed the way she ran the office.

Hell. He missed her. Period.

Scott reentered the office, this time carrying a small paperback book.

"You should read this." He tossed the novel on the desk and sat down. "It's Deborah's latest release, and it's all about you."

Daniel stared at the book that lay cover up, showing a man in a business suit embracing a beautiful brunette. "Deborah wrote this? I thought her writing was just a hobby."

"She's quite good, too," Vincent said. "When Scott told me about it, I picked up a copy for myself."

"You read this?"

"I sure did."

"Caroline did, too. She was the one who found it," Scott said. "She was at Deborah's house, and her computer was displaying her author page."

Daniel picked up the book and read the author's name. "Janine Gott."

"She writes under a pen name," Scott said. "The romance is erotic, and I don't think she ever intended for anyone she knows to discover it."

Daniel flipped through the pages, noticing the length of the book and that several passages were highlighted in fluorescent yellow marker. The novel was well over three hundred pages. "You read it?"

"God, no." Scott shook his head and took his seat. "Caroline did—cover to cover. She highlighted the more…" he smirked, and then added, "Let's just say, she marked the more intriguing and revealing parts."

The phrase "Of course, sir" repeated and highlighted caught Daniel's attention. In the margin, the phrase was translated in Caroline's handwriting as "I love you."

It was Deborah's book. She'd written each word, had contacted an agent, and had had it published. Daniel stroked the book's spine. She had been in love with him since, at least, the start of writing it.

"This is her second book in a series of billionaire romances," Scott said.

Good Lord. She had loved him since the start of the *first* book? Years. She had loved him for years.

Vincent pointed at the novel in Daniel's hands. "This is a woman who takes great pride in her work, is very dedicated, and extremely loyal." After a brief pause, he added, "You can add talented, as well."

"She is all that." Daniel rubbed his brow and felt tiny beads of sweat. His mouth also felt dry.

She was more than that and he knew it. A true soul mate.

"Do you love her?" Scott asked.

Daniel swallowed the lump in his throat. He had never considered Deborah in such a way before, but a heaviness in his heart at the thought of her no longer coming into the office every day, of not seeing her... It felt too hard to bear.

He bit his lip as his brow furrowed. All he could think about was their night together and how right everything had seemed.

Taking the book in his hands once again, he flipped through it. This time, he read the notes in the margins in more detail. A fancy dinner and an art gallery opening were commented upon. On the blank page in the back of the novel, some dates and what dresses the character wore in the book were written. In particular, a red, strapless gown was mentioned.

Deborah had worn such a dress on one of their dates. "What's all this?"

"That was my idea," Vincent admitted. "When Scott and Caroline told me about the book, I suggested they somehow recreate the more romantic scenes to see if Deborah would admit how much she cares for you."

"Caroline initially wanted to set you up on a blind date with each other..."

Daniel's gaze darted to Scott.

"Deborah's clothes, the opera, the dinner... Caroline recreated all the romantic scenes as best she could from the book. You choosing Deborah to pretend to be your wife was the best opportunity we could have asked for. It set the stage so you could discover for yourself how deeply in love you are with her."

His eyes narrowed. "What made you think I'd take the bait?"

"Oh, not to worry." An evil smirk crossed Scott's face, a smirk that reminded Daniel of their earlier working days together—when the two would target a failing company and go in for the kill. "I had an insurance policy."

Daniel let out a deep breath. Scott knew him so well and understood what made him tick. "What the hell are you talking about?"

"Ms. Ortiz." Scott chuckled, and the smile that spread across his face told Daniel that he was pleased with himself. "I found the worst secretary at the temp agency and made sure she was assigned to you."

Daniel bolted upright in his chair. "That incompetent gold digger was your doing?"

"Oh, she really *is* all that bad. I just made sure she was sent to our human resources department. Next, I called in a favor from Ravi."

"Who's Ravi?" Vincent asked.

"My doctor." Daniel said the answer quickly and kept his gaze on Scott. "What did Ravi do?"

"I asked him to negatively highlight Ms. Ortiz's lesser qualities so you could see how wonderful Deborah is."

Daniel nodded his head in a critical way, with his

arms crossed. "You know he slept with that piece of work on my plane."

Scott cleared his throat. "Ravi went off script with that one."

Daniel lowered his head and thought about the flight. A sinking feeling hit him in his gut. "What about the boy Evan? Did you arrange for him too?"

"The new hire?" Scott shook his head. "I haven't met him yet."

Daniel eyed Scott critically, but knew he told the truth. Evan was genuine, he was certain of that.

He took a deep breath and closed his eyes as he slumped back into the cushion of his leather chair. They had set him up. His best friends and his father... They... He opened his eyes and glared from one man to the other, their hopeful expressions melting away any anger he felt. They knew him so well. How could he be upset?

And, he did care for Deborah. He gripped the book tightly and a warmth spread throughout his heart. "I do love her." He heard the words as he said them and a tear welled up in his eye. "If I don't tell her soon, I'm going to lose her forever."

He looked pleadingly at them. Knowing how terrible everything turned out after their night together, he confessed, "I've messed up everything."

"You haven't, son." Vincent pointed to the book, his face filled with fatherly love. "She loves you."

Scott nodded. "She says so every time she speaks the words, 'Of course, sir.'"

The trigger phrase pulsed his heart rate faster. How many times each day did she say that to him?

He needed some air.

No, he needed *her*.

"Read that novel," Scott said. "It'll tell you everything you need to know."

28

*D*eborah made herself another cup of coffee and stared at the bottle of brandy on her kitchen table. She'd bought the alcohol when her son left for college since she'd found that a nightcap soothed her in the empty house. The time was technically after high noon, so no one could claim she was boozing it, but it was still too early to drink.

"Alcohol isn't going to solve your problems." Her sister Sue walked into the kitchen and picked up the bottle. She tightened the cap back and studied the label before placing it back on top of the refrigerator. "I didn't even know you had a bottle of Disaronno."

Her one bottle of hard liquor. She glanced at the tiny bottle—the smallest one Disaronno came in—and noted the small amount of golden liquor gone. She had used so little, you could almost swear she had only now opened it.

"Why don't you take a shower and we can go out to lunch?" Sue said, her voice too cheery for Deborah. "The sky is blue, and it's a beautiful day."

Was it Wednesday? Thursday? Deborah didn't even know anymore.

Not that it mattered.

She slowly shuck her head and shuffled in her house shoes to the kitchen table where she plopped into a chair. She should try to get dressed today, she should get something to eat, she...she should have never let her sister in the door.

Running to her that first night was one thing, but Sue had called or come over every single day since. It was sweet of her to care, but it interfered with Deborah's all-day crying plans.

"Deb, I'm concerned." Sue scanned the room. "Sink full of dishes, your mail unopened on the table..." She now focused on Deborah and the sloppy atire she was in. "And you." She took a seat next to her sister, her arm around her shoulder and her hand gently stroking her unkempt hair. "You're a mess."

A week had passed since Deborah had last seen Daniel, although he had called several times. Biting her lip, she kept her tears at bay. She didn't want to cry any more over something she never had. She certainly hadn't expected Mr. Ellington to give up his carefree lifestyle to chase down a secretary.

An ex–secretary.

An unemployed, ex–secretary, who had not heard

about the scholarship being renewed for her son. So an unemployed and *penniless* ex–secretary. A woman who missed her target objective since Daniel had still made it to the top of that damn list.

She was pathetic.

"I'm sorry that things with your boss didn't work out." Deborah's phone buzzed from the kitchen counter where it was charging, the familiar ring tone signaling it was Daniel and not Josh—both of whom had called her several times.

"He keeps calling." Sue retrieved the phone and brought it over. Looking at the display, she added, "Josh texted too. He wants to know if you're all right." She handed the phone to Deb, but she wouldn't take it.

She didn't want to talk to her son right now. What was she supposed to say? Get another job because I suck as a mother and lost your hard-earned scholarship? Maybe she could confront Daniel and have him make good on the their deal, even though she completely failed on her end.

Ugh! That would mean having to see him. She didn't want to go back to that office. Definitely didn't want to go back to his home. Other than officially turning her resignation in, she shouldn't have to go through the humiliation.

Sue texted on Deborah's phone. "I'm telling Josh you're doing better. He's wondering if he should change his spring break plans and come home so…"

"No." Good Lord, she didn't need him doing a marathon drive to Chicago during a busy drive-time like spring break. Every college kid was on the road, as well as families traveling across the country. Plus, Josh had been asked by a friend to vacation at a beach-front resort. He had been so excited, especially since the hotel was already paid for by his friend and all Josh had to expense was the gas money. He needed this vacation, especially after working so hard this semester. "Tell him I'm fine and not to come home."

Sue texted and hit send. She then placed the phone back on the charge station and began cleaning the mail and paperwork off the table. "Perhaps a trip out there to see him would do you some good. The problem is that you've been cooped up in your house for days."

No, the real problem was her and Daniel's one–night stand which caused her to hide out. Why did she cave? She had remained strong for nearly two decades, and because of a silly diamond ring on her hand, she'd become a love–struck girl willing to spread her legs and sleep with her boss.

She was as weak as the heroines of her book series.

Billionaire bosses were married to their businesses and obsessed with the rush they felt with mergers and takeovers. The love of a good woman was only something they enjoyed for thirty minutes in bed before they kicked you out.

Which was exactly what had happened except she and Daniel had made love for hours, and, technically, she was the one who left their bed—and in such a rush. What could he possibly be thinking of her? They enjoy a passionate night together and then she goes all crazy?

Geez, he always said he did his best to avoid the psychos out there, and here she was—one of the crazies that came out of the woodwork. The man couldn't have even seen this coming since she had kept her secret so well.

But, secrets or not, she hadn't learned anything from the affair nearly twenty years ago. So, she was a slut *and* an idiot.

A cry escaped her throat, and she did her best to stifle it. Her night with Daniel meant so much more to her than just a tryst. She had sacrificed her professional life with him for a one–night stand that was no more than him satisfying an itch. He'd toss her aside and move on, just like his uncle had done.

Her cell phone chirped, and she ignored it once again. It was Daniel. What did he want? To tell her that he needed her for the merger? That the office was a mess without her? Would it just be business as usual, or would he want a quick fling on the couch in his office for a few weeks and then show her to the door?

She couldn't even handle looking into his beautiful blue eyes any more. She would see that he got what he had wanted, and then those gorgeous eyes would gaze upon another woman—probably in her twenties—and Deborah would be asked to send herself a parting gift.

"That's it." Sue grouped all the dishes so they were at least all around the sink and waiting to be cleaned. She then tugged at Deborah's arm. "We're going out to lunch."

Deborah shrugged her off. "Maybe tomorrow. I think I'll go back to bed."

Sue's eyes narrowed, and one hand rested on her hip. "I'm not going to have you wither away like this. Go upstairs, shower, and get dressed." When Deborah didn't answer, Sue added, "Listen Didi. I'm sorry things didn't work out between you and your boss. But you need to get your life back in order."

The word boss echoed in her mind. He was now her ex-boss.

"I know. Things happen. It's just life." Deborah had been saying that a lot to herself in an effort to believe it and move on. Deep down, she knew the expression wasn't working.

Still wearing her pajamas, she was slowly becoming the clichéd, unemployed bum, who let themselves go with no plan or hope for the future. Invites like having lunch with your sister were important. She just didn't want to eat today.

Wasn't that the epitome of being a couch potato?

Sue pointed to the stack of paperwork on the

kitchen table she had just cleaned up. "You don't have to go see the man, but you should mail in your resignation later and then go file for unemployment. We should go to the Workforce Commission and see the job postings."

She really shouldn't let another day slip by. Besides, now that she wasn't employed by Ellington–Weston, she wasn't receiving a paycheck, and Josh wouldn't be getting the next installment of his scholarship. She couldn't afford to be a lazy bum.

Picking up the resignation letter which rested atop the stack. She sealed the envelop and grabbed a pen. "I'll mail it today." Her heart ached. She wasn't just leaving Daniel, she really did love her job. She never thought she'd walk away from it.

"That's the spirit." Sue said in a happy tone. "Go shower and get dressed. I'll clean this kitchen and straighten the house."

Deborah stood. Lunch, resignation, then find another job. Deborah had picked herself up once before. She could do it again.

29

*D*aniel once again checked the video feeds of his home security cameras. The pictures buzzed to life on the monitors in his home office, showing him that, at dark–thirty in the morning, the stalking women already held their posts by his gate.

The dwindling crowd proved to be hardcore. Some women stayed the night in the cold, and more arrived early the next morning to stalk him. Overall, there was a constant few dozen positioned at his gate at all times.

Such a nuisance.

He couldn't even read a book in peace in his own home. Each time he glanced out a window he saw them spring to life, cameras ready, and shouting his name.

Did women really think such a ploy would help them land a rich man? Were they looking for anything more than just to be treated to an overflowing bank account? Couldn't they see that the were transparent in their desires and that no man would consider themselves lucky to have such attention?

At the very least, his security gate held them back several feet away from his house. If it weren't for the iron bars, he suspected a few of them might have tried to enter his home for a personal, private tour.

Like that would ever happen.

He needed to modify his daily commute to work again or stay in. He had stayed away from the office the last few days, but he should meet with people in regards to his company's merger.

Work was always there. It'd be there tomorrow, too.

He felt a tightening in his chest. Days had passed and the pain of her loss was still as bad as the day she left.

Screw the merger. He needed a personal day.

Dressed in comfortable jeans and a white, button–down shirt, he didn't want to fight the crowd of women who lined the entry of his office building every morning, and he specifically wanted to avoid hiring another damn temp secretary.

He grabbed Deborah's book from his desk and thumbed through it, causing the mailed–in resignation she had sent him—which he used as a bookmark—to tumble to the ground. She couldn't even call him. She'd just sent him a letter confirming that she'd quit.

The yellow highlighted areas he had marked in the book colored the pages, and he had written more notes in the margin. Sections of the story mirrored his real life, or, at least, the dates he had gone on when he'd pretended to be engaged to Deborah. The last section of the novel, where the billionaire hero proposes to his assistant, was a part of the novel he had read repeatedly.

A whine came from Oreo and he jumped up to lick Daniel's face.

"I'm okay, buddy."

Ginger now woke from her spot on the floor and followed her brother's suit. The two hadn't left his side in days.

They knew he was unhappy, and like all dogs, they wanted to lick away the sorrow and make him happy once again.

Daniel patted both on the head and held them at bay, his face now dripping with puppy saliva. "I'm just a little nervous. You don't have to worry about me. In fact, I'm going to make all of our lives better."

Mentally checking for the items he would need, he walked into his kitchen. Getting a dozen red roses home from a florist shop was next to impossible, but easier than having a flower truck pull up in front of his house and drop them off. The last thing he needed was to be featured on any more social media postings.

The long box of flowers barely fit in his refrigerator, even with one of the sliding shelves removed. He took out the long, slender container and set it on the kitchen counter so he could place the ribbon directly in the center. It was too early for champagne, so he went to his wine cooler and pulled out the sparkling apple cider he had placed there last night.

Armed with the book, her resignation, the flowers, and the fake champagne, he grabbed the keys to Scott's Tesla and made his way into the garage. Borrowing his friend's car yesterday was the only way he had managed to get to the florist undetected, but he wasn't too sure about driving an entirely electric car.

The car unlocked as he approached, and he placed the items in his hand into the back seat.

He climbed in and started the car, appreciating how quiet the engine sounded. If it weren't for the interior lights, he would never have guessed that the car was running.

It seemed to be the perfect getaway car.

He slowly crept out of the garage. As he approached the entry gate to his estate, he saw a few cold women spring to life and shout his name.

He pulled onto the highway and followed the GPS guiding system. The morning traffic had not begun yet, and he made good time. Deborah's neighborhood only now buzzed to life with early morning commuters.

He drove from one quaint street to the next in a maze–like fashion until he reached her avenue. She owned the green house on the corner. The grass in the lawn fought its way through the patches of snow. Two wicker chairs sat on the porch with a table in between. If he had to guess which house on this block was hers, he would have chosen this one. Not because he knew her so well, but because the house was a setting in her book. It was where the hero had proposed to the heroine in a very *Pretty Woman* movie sort of way.

The movie had always seemed so trite to him, but women loved it.

Now that he understood what love was, he under the movie's appeal.

Her car still sat in the driveway, so he parked behind her. If things went poorly, she wouldn't be able to leave in a huff. He took a deep breath as he remained in the car one more minute with the keys in his hand.

Over the last few days, he'd managed to read her book. He hated romance novels, but this one nearly read like a diary of his life.

Naturally, the gallery scene in her second book— very much like the opera they had attended—and the scene at his office hadn't played out quite the same in real life. She hadn't been on the floor of the two locations moaning out his name...but maybe they could play out the story's last scene.

He walked up the walk to the front door. This would be their fairy tale ending. Their happily ever after.

At least he hoped so.

Deborah didn't have time to thoroughly dry her hair before getting dressed and checking her daily planner once again for the address of the unemployment agency. She wanted to arrive just as they opened their doors so she could cross the unpleasant chore of standing in a line and begging for money off her to–do list.

Her only real skill was secretarial. Perhaps she would be lucky and find a female executive to work for. If she couldn't find something ideal, she could hire on with a temp agency.

She didn't want to do temp work, but she wasn't in a position to be picky about where her next paycheck came from. The unemployment agency would have a list of the temp places she could apply to, as well as possibly other companies she hadn't even thought about.

Of course, she didn't need to be someone's assistant. Once her son graduated college, she could go back and finish her degree. She could start over in a different field, that was if her writing didn't take off and provide a living for her.

She closed her eyes and a shiver ran down her spine. She wasn't going to succeed as an author and she knew it. Writing two and a half books within the span of several years and then publishing them with mediocre sales would not sustain her. No one knew she wrote—which is how she wanted it—but she needed better sales.

She'd just grabbed her purse and keys off the table when she heard the doorbell ring. She wasn't expecting company, so she walked to the door and peered out the peephole.

It was Daniel.

A slight gasp escaped her throat and it felt like all the air had escaped out of the room.

She hadn't seen him in days. He had never visited her home before, but she assumed this visit was due to her official resignation letter she had mailed in. She had hoped he would call to say goodbye, but she hadn't expected him to make a personal trip to see her.

She hadn't even heard his car pull up. Instinctively, her hand brushed through her still damp hair before she opened the door.

"Hello, Deborah."

Glancing away, she found it difficult to look the man in the eyes. He stood before her in jeans and a button–down shirt, his comfort wardrobe for when he wasn't at work. Since it was a workday, he must have made a special trip just for her and wasn't planning to go into the office.

But that was the butterflies and the hope she carried within her talking.

He hadn't said much to her since the night they had spent together, and she knew his usual routine. His parade of women typically received flowers the day after having sex with him, a phone call two days later, a dinner invite for the following Friday, and a small gift of jewelry or other personal item wrapped and mailed to them. It was all rote.

She didn't want to be clumped into the bevy of young girls he chose to sleep with, and there had been no flowers or dinner invites. Obviously, she wasn't worthy of his usual routine. But, then again, she regularly took care of the details of scheduling his love life. It seemed silly to send herself any of those things, knowing they didn't really come from him.

"Deborah, may I come in."

Daniel's smile caused his baby blue eyes to twinkle, and he looked happier than she had seen him in a long time.

The man was actually happy? Happy to be rid of her?

Against her best judgment, she opened the door and gestured for him to enter. Her home wasn't as grand as his, and she certainly didn't have a foyer. The front door opened directly into the living room of her tiny three-bedroom house.

He carried in a long floral box, which had to be held sidewise for him to enter. "These are for you."

She took the long, white box from his hands, knowing full well that it contained long–stemmed roses. The packaging seemed a bit old fashioned, but she'd always thought a presentation of flowers in such a manner was romantic. Which was why her heroines' love interests presented them with such flowers in her novels.

She had only once before received long–stemmed roses packaged like this, but it wasn't a romantic gesture. It was when she had given birth to Josh, and Carl had signed the card congratulating her on the birth of her son. *Her* son, not *their* son or even *his*.

Her hands shook as she held the white container. This was the thank–you–for–the–sex gift that she would always send out to Daniel's past loves.

Step one. Check.

She led Daniel into the kitchen. She placed the gift on the counter, and her fingers fumbled nervously with the red bow until it finally untied and she could freely pull the ribbon from the box.

Inside lay a dozen long–stemmed red roses. Beautiful, perfect, unwanted.

"You should get them into water," he said.

"Of course, sir." She bit her lip as she heard the words escape.

Habit. Just a force of habit. She took a deep breath and noticed him staring at her.

The wide grin that spread across his face told her something was up, but she was no longer his secretary, and this parting gift said as much.

Step two was a piece of jewelry. A nice shiny

bauble that basically said, "here's something shiny to keep your attention while I make my getaway."

She wasn't ready to see step two.

"I assume you received my letter of resignation." She opened a cabinet and retrieved a large vase. Any change of topic, even the loss of her job, was better.

He pulled the envelope from his back pocket and tossed it on the counter. "I don't accept it."

She stared at the white envelope with the office address and recognized her handwriting. She couldn't bring herself to face him, so mailing the notice in, however impersonal, seemed like the best option.

"I also renewed the scholarship for Josh."

The rock at the pit of her stomach lifted and she found it easier to breath. Her gaze met his. At least she had that, regardless that she had left.

Thank God. Josh would be okay.

"Thank you." She had hoped to see hurt in Daniel's eyes or at the very least some type of loss at her leaving, but no. His expression remained calm while she felt a tightening in her chest and just wanted to escape. "Josh and I appreciate it."

She walked away from him. With shaky hands, she turned on the water and filled the vase. "The roses are lovely." Her voice was wavering, so she took a deep breath and tried to keep the conversation professional. "May I count on you as a reference for my next job?"

"Are you so eager to leave me, Ms. Woodrow?"

She froze at hearing him call her by the name of the heroine in her novel and quoting a line from the story. A flurry of emotions flooded her thoughts—the most dominant one being embarrassment—as she nearly dropped the vase into the sink. She felt her cheeks flush and her knees grow weak.

He knew.

She turned off the water and slowly spun around. Daniel was on one knee. The diamond of his grandmother's ring caught the kitchen light and sparkled brightly in the box he held open.

She couldn't breathe.

He knew about her book. He knew about…about her love for him.

His outfit, the roses…this was the last chapter of her novel.

"I read one of your books."

Her mouth had gone dry as she backed up and her hips bumped into the sink.

"All these years, I didn't see you. You blended in and became my right–hand man for so long that I didn't notice you—not until you weren't there anymore." He licked his lips and held up the ring. "I see you now, Deborah, and I like what I see. You are intelligent and kind, thoughtful and loyal. You compliment me and make me want to be a better person."

How long had she wanted this moment to happen? How many ways had she imagined it? A tear rolled down her cheek, and before she could wipe it away, he drew a handkerchief from his pocket and handed it to her.

"I want to be there for you," he said as she accepted the offering. "I want you to continue being there for me. I need you to be at my side because I can't live without you. You are my everything. Please marry me."

Wiping away her tears, she realized she had been holding her breath, but she managed to say, "Of course, sir."

The End

Thank you for reading "Bachelor Heart" of the "Rich Indulgence" series.

To find out more about Lawyer Scott Hollister in "Bachelor Soul," please visit http://www.reginamorris.com/bachelor-soul-info

To find out more about Doctor Ravi Amarro in "Bachelor in Love," please visit http://www. reginamorris.com/bachelor-in-love-info

To leave a review for "Bachelor Heart" at the retailer where you purchased the book, please visit http:// www.reginamorris.com/bachelor-heart-info

ABOUT THE AUTHOR

Dear Readers,

I hope you enjoyed reading my novel, Bachelor Heart, book 1 in the 3-part book series 'Rich Indulgence'. Please leave a review on the retailer site where you purchased the book.

You can find a link to all retailers at: reginamorris.com/bachelor-heart.

Please visit my website (http://www. reginamorris.com) for more information about my other novels and short stories. A list of my books and descriptions are below.

Please feel free to contact me through my website, through my many social media sites (see my website for the a list) or by email at mailto:regina@ reginamorris.com?subject=Email from fan.

I like to play games and have fun in my quarterly electronic newsletters. Please sign up at newsletter.reginamorris.com

By day, I work in a small cubicle as a computer programmer, but at night I write about vampires, billionaires, and other romance combinations. I capture my creativity on the pages of my passionate stories. I write about second chance romances, mature romances (where the characters are 40+ years of age), and about vampires.

My contemporary romances are mostly sweet romances (please check descriptions to confirm). The romances build a connection between two people with happily-ever-afters. No cliff-hangers, but complete stories.

The books in my series are all stand-alone novels that can be read in any order.

My COLONY series is about vampires who can alter their aged appearances by the amount of blood they consume. The series is about a covert team of sexy vampires who protect the President of the United States. This series' success prompted me to launch another series ("COLONY World") that involves the same world, but about civilian vampires who live among unsuspecting humans.

The heat level differs from mild to hot in my books. My stories involving the Historical Preservation Agency and time travel are mild. My COLONY series, COLONY World series, and some of my contemporary romances are hot. These hot stories have an age warning of 18+ on them. My contemporary short stories are mild. My contemporary novels vary.

I live in Austin, Texas with my husband and two children. I graduated high school in Germany and I attended the University of Texas at Austin, where I *received a degree in Computer Science with a minor in math. After enjoying a career in software engineering, I discovered that writing is in my blood, and had to put pen to paper!*

The opinions I express in my novels are my own. My stories are my own intellectual property. Copyright (c) 2012-2021, Regina Morris

Sincerely,
Regina Morris

ACKNOWLEDGMENTS

Special thanks to my husband and our children for their love and support; to my sister for believing in me and encouraging me to follow my dreams; to my critique partners, Jean and Pennie, for being with me every step of the way; to my editor Chelle (Literally Addicted to Detail); and my proof reader team. I also want to thank my beta readers, and street team. This book would not be possible without the support I have had from all of you.

Contemporary Romance Novels

Christmas in Newbury: A Billionaire Dad & Nanny
Romance

ISBN: 978–1–948997–47–8 (Epub Ebook)

ISBN: 978–1–948997–48–5 (MOBI Ebook)

ISBN: 978–1–948997–49–2 (Paperback)

Audio as well

Billionaire James Nielson plans to close many of his
business's installations, including the original factory
started by his grandfather in the small town of
Newbury, when a woman—whom he had a sexual fling
with over a year ago—abandons her baby at his company's
headquarters claiming he is the father.

He and his baby daughter visit Newbury during the
holidays where he hires a local woman, Melanie Frank, to
be his nanny. She has been furloughed from her job at his
factory, and, like everyone in the town, relies on the
company for her livelihood. She wants to be an artist, but
is financially trapped in the town by the company.

It is obvious to Melanie that James is uneasy around his
daughter, isn't finding the town charming, and doesn't feel
any Christmas spirit. She's plenty attracted to James, but

will this city mouse really be interested in a country mouse? As James discovers lost family members, the warmth of a small community spirit, and the compassion from his daughter's nanny, he develops a stronger sense of family and his romantic feelings for Melanie grow.

He decides he must keep the factory running, and after buying Melanie's artwork at the local Christmas auction, she has renewed interest in her studies. The two search for the perfect Christmas gift for each other while trying to save the factory, which leads to a Christmas miracle.

Contemporary Sweet Romance Short Stories

Taking Chances

978–0–9966192–9–5 (ebook)

Available as an audio book

Broken engagement, a disappointed father, an emotional mother, what else could a wounded soldier ask for? Tommy has no idea that his sweet nurse remembers him prior to his injuries. Always professional, Abby treats Tommy no differently because of their awkward past. Once the truth is out, what will become of their friendship and budding romance?

* * *

Christmas Joy

978–1–948997–18–8 (MOBI)

978–1–948997–19–5 (ePub)

978–1–948997–20–1 (Paperback)

Jake needs to clear out his father's old cabin and sell it.

He's prepared to deal with the freezing cold weather and the remote location, but not with the sexy woman, who was once his late father's nurse, still living in the place.

* * *

More Than Puppy Love

978–1–948997–01–0 (MOBI)

978–1–948997–02–7 (ePub)

978–1–948997–03–4 (Paperback)

Ex-wallflower, now veterinarian, Kacie Preston is eager to go to her ten-year high school reunion where she can meet up with the boy she crushed on for years. But then his dog, her patient, shows up at the event mistreated. How well does Kacie really know her old heart throb?

* * *

FANASY / TIME TRAVEL BOOKS

Just in Time (Short Story - Prequel to Time Historian)

ISBN: 978–0–9966192–5–7 (ebook)

ISBN: 978–0–9966192–6–4 (paperback)

Managing teams to send recorders back in history is stressful enough, but when the government makes a play for proprietary technology from the Historical Preservation Agency, Caleb must rely upon a well-connected, and sexy, developer at a government agency for help. Can the two of them keep time travel in the hands of historians?

* * *

Time Historian

ISBN: 978–0–9966192–8–8 (Print)

ISBN: 978–0–9966192–7–1 (ebook)

Also available as an audio book

Hank McConnell's is having a bad day at the office. First, he just destroyed history. He finds himself living in the Confederate States of America, Lincoln was convicted as a war criminal, and slavery existed for another fifty years. Secondly, his blunder erased his family from existence and his alternate self works as a lonely tenured professor instead of at the Historical Preservation Agency.

He doesn't have much time. He travels back to Lincoln's presidency to right what went wrong. Unfortunately, correcting time is like herding cats and one fix leads to more and more changes.

Is he willing to do the unthinkable to make the world whole again?

PARANORMAL (VAMPIRE) ROMANCES

COLONY Series Books

Vampires exist among us. They can be our neighbor, our best friend, our child's teacher…

They alter their aged appearance based upon the amount of blood they consume. They move to a new area, drink a lot of blood, and appear young. Slowly they limit their intake of blood and age, right in front of our unsuspecting eyes. After decades, they fake their death, move, and do it over and over again.

Most live quiet lives in an effort to blend in.

Some, however, want power and control.

The COLONY is an elite group of vampires sworn to protect the President of the United States from these rogue vampires. Few humans are privileged to this knowledge.

* * *

Eternal Service (Book #1)

Top 100 Bestseller

978–0–9888222–0–7 (ebook)

978–0–9888222–1–4 (paperback)

Available as an audio book

Vampire Raymond Metcalf has too many balls to juggle and life is getting more complicated by the minute. As if working with a covert team of sexy vampires to protect the President isn't enough, he has to deal with his rebellious half-breed son, save the President from a crazed vampire, and break in a new director for his team since the last one, his best friend and the only human he trusts, has decided to retire. Why does his friend's replacement have to be the most beautiful human woman Raymond has ever seen?

Career military woman, Alex Brennan, is being offered the promotion of a lifetime, and with it a romance that she has desperately been seeking. Does she dare accept the position as Director of the COLONY, an elite group of deadly creatures of the night and risk a dangerous romance with a man who isn't even human? Together, can they save the President?

* * *

United Service (Book #2)

Top 100 Bestseller

978–0–9888222–6–9 (ebook)

978–0–9888222–7–6 (paperback)

Available as an audio book

Sterling Metcalf is a modern–day vampire who clashes with his father's antiquated ideals. Being the half–breed of the COLONY group, Sterling hates being the team's weakest link. He jumps at an opportunity to do some fieldwork rescuing kidnapped vampire children and is accompanied by Kate Spencer, the nanny of one of the children.

Kate is a purebred vampire with a secret of her own. Can Sterling put aside his bad–boy ways and woo the lovely Kate? Will Kate accept the advances of a half–breed? Together, can they save the children from a religious cult who wants to kill them?

* * *

Enduring Service (Book #3)

Top 100 Bestseller

978–0–9914034–0–0 (ebook)

978–0–9914034–1–7 (paperback)

Available as an audio book

Colony Agent Sulie Metcalf, the President's private physician, has been in love with the same human man for nearly thirty years. She refuses to allow herself the joy of true love because her feelings are unrequited by her human boss, Jonathan Dixon. As Dixon's retirement looms near, and his memories of Sulie and the last thirty years of his life are about to be erased, does she confront her fear of intimacy and take a leap of faith before it's too late?

Dixon has decided to retire and enjoy what time he has left. When his best friend Sulie, a vampire team member, is kidnapped during a medical emergency, Dixon realizes that retirement means giving up everything, and everyone, he's known for the last three decades. Will he risk his life, and his heart, to save her?

* * *

Equality of Service (Book #4)

978–1–948997–07–2 (MOBI)

978–1–948997–08–9 (ePub)

978–1–948997–09–6 (paperback)

Available as an audio book

Fifteen years ago, COLONY Agent William Wardell met his future wife Jackie Pearlman. She's sexy, opinionated, and finds him to be a mockery of the American dream of equality for all.

Can a past Freedom Rider and racial activist from the 1960s, now turned vampire, prove to the love of his life that he's not a political puppet?

* * *

Reliant Service (Book #5)

978–0–9914034–2–4 (ebook)

978–0–9914034–3–1 (paperback)

Available as an audio book

After faking his death from an assassination attempt on the President, and retiring his first and only alias with the COLONY, Daniel Brighton discovers the mandatory sabbatical to be less than exciting. He chooses to do a favor and act as a security guard for a fading pop–singer, Lori Austin, whose career is winding down. He travels across Europe with her and discovers her past to be one of deception and intrigue with a history leading directly back to the COLONY itself.

Lori Austin is struggling to keep her career alive, and is willing to do what is necessary to save it. From bad press and scandalous stories, she travels across Europe on a relief tour to revitalize her career, but doesn't realize she is traveling with a vampire. Discovering a hidden family secret, she realizes that the one man who can save her is the handsome security guard she fought so hard not to hire.

* * *

Echo of Service (Book #6)

ISBN: 978–1–948997–31–7 (EPub Ebook)

ISBN: 978–1–948997–32–4 (MOBI Ebook)

ISBN: 978–1–948997–33–1 (Paperback)

Also available as an audio book

After the President of the United States is poisoned, Vampire COLONY agent Mason Warner steps in as the man's double. He manages the President's hectic schedule just fine until the political party sends in a public relations expert to clean up the President's image. She is the one woman from Mason's past whom he has never forgotten— the woman who is the measuring stick he compares all other women too—but he compelled her decades ago to forget their one night together.

Nicole Banner is assigned by the party to do a makeover on the one man from her past she despises the most. Years ago, her short-lived secret fling with the Senator of Massachusetts, now President of the United States, left her with a son to raise on her own.

Mason can't risk her remembering their tryst from decades ago since she believes him to be the President. Nicole has always hidden her affair from prying eyes, until now.

He still desires her. All she wants is revenge.

COLONY World Series Books

These vampire romances feature vampires from the COLONY world, but these vampires do not work for the government.

* * *

Winter Wishes (Book #1)

ISBN: 978–0–9981866–0–3 (ebook)

ISBN: 978–0–9981866–1–0 (paperback)

Available as an audio book

Sammy needs a holiday miracle. The Vampire Council is after him, he's falling in love with his best friend's mother–in–law, and there's artwork hanging on the wall that was stolen by the Nazis. Life is spiraling out of control for this Jewish vampire as he spends the Christmas holiday baking cookies and wrapping gifts for the needy.

Louise is busy with her charities and hosting her annual

Christmas party. Putting a smile on her face proves difficult when her soon to be ex–husband arrives with a bimbo on his arm, her proposed divorce settlement is far from fair, and the sexy stranger she's starting to fall for believes she's a Nazi.

* * *

Destined Desire (Book #2)

ISBN: 978–1–948997–16–4 (EPub ebook)

ISBN: 978–1–948997–15–7 (MOBI ebook)

ISBN: 978–1–948997–17–1 (paperback)

Available as an audio book

After a car accident nearly kills his immortal father, Alexander rushes to his father's side only to discover that his parents want him to marry and stay closer to home. He's already been down this path once before with a less than desirable outcome, so he refuses. He's steadfast in his decision until his parents threaten to financially cut him off and he's forced to approach the Vampire Council for a new marriage contract.

Dionora is enjoying her new job at the Vampire Council Marriage Office. The holidays take an exciting turn for her when she discovers the next match she does is for her ex–fiancé.

Revenge is sweet with this sensual romantic comedy.